THE BOY
WITH THE
CUCKOO-CLOCK
HEART

THE BOY WITH THE CUCKOO-CLOCK HEART

· Mathias Malzieu ·

Translated from the French by SARAH ARDIZZONE

ALFRED A. KNOPF · New York · 2010

THIS IS A BORZOI BOOK
PUBLISHED BY ALFRED A. KNOPF

Originally published in France as
La Mécanique du coeur
by Flammarion, Paris, in 2007.
Copyright © 2007 by Flammarion.
This translation originally published in
Great Britain by Chatto & Windus,
the Random House Group Ltd.,
London, in 2009.

Library of Congress Cataloging-in-Publication Data
Malzieu, Mathias.
[Mécanique du coeur. English]
The boy with the cuckoo-clock heart / Mathias Malzieu ;
translated from the French by Sarah Ardizzone. —1st U.S. ed.
p. cm.
Translated from the French.
ISBN 978-0-307-27168-6
1. Heart, Artificial—Fiction.   2. Magic realism (Literature)
I. Ardizzone, Sarah, 1970–   II. Title.
PQ2713.A374M4313 2010
843'.92—dc22   2009044793

Manufactured in the United States of America
First United States Edition

For you Acacita, who made this book grow in my belly

FIRSTLY: *don't touch the hands of your cuckoo-clock heart.* **SECONDLY:** *master your anger.* **THIRDLY:** *never, ever fall in love. For if you do, the hour hand will poke through your skin, your bones will shatter, and your heart will break once more.*

THE **BOY**
WITH THE
CUCKOO-CLOCK
HEART

chapter one

In which Little Jack is born on the coldest day on earth and miraculously resuscitated

It's snowing over Edinburgh on this 16th day of April, 1874. An eerie, freezing cold gridlocks the city. Old people wonder whether this might be the coldest day on earth. The sun seems to have disappeared for good. There's a biting wind, snowflakes lighter than air. WHITE! WHITE! WHITE! A muffled explosion. This is all we can see. Houses resemble steam engines, as the gray smoke exhaled by their chimneys sparkles in the steel sky.

Edinburgh and its steep streets are being transformed. Fountains metamorphose, one by one, into bouquets of ice. The old river, usually so serious, is disguised as an icing sugar lake that stretches all the way to the sea. The din of the surf rings out like the sound of windows smashing. Miraculously, the hoarfrost stitches sequins on to cats' bodies. The trees stretch their arms, like fat fairies in white nightshirts yawning at the moon, as they watch the carriages sliding over the cobblestone ice rink. It is so cold that birds freeze in midflight before crashing to the ground. The noise as they drop out of the sky is uncannily soft for a corpse.

This is the coldest day on earth. And I'm getting ready to be born.

The scene is an old house perched on top of the highest hill in Edinburgh, Arthur's Seat; that King's remains are supposed to lie at the top of this sleeping volcano set in blue quartz. The roof of the house is ingeniously pitched and pointy. The chimney, shaped like a butcher's knife, underscores the stars. The moon sharpens its quarters here. There's nobody around, just trees.

Inside, everything is made of wood, as if the house had been carved from an enormous pine tree. It's like walking into a log cabin: ruggedly exposed beams, tiny windows rescued from the train scrapyard, and a low table hewn from a single stump. Woollen cushions stuffed with dead leaves complete the nestlike atmosphere. Numerous clandestine births are carried out in this house.

Here lives strange Dr. Madeleine, the midwife—otherwise

known as "that mad-wife" by the city's residents—who is on the pretty side for an old lady. She still has a glint in her eye, but her smile is just a twitch, betraying a loose connection in her facial wiring.

Dr. Madeleine brings into the world the children of prostitutes and abandoned women, who are too young or too unfaithful to give birth the conventional way. As well as helping with new life, Dr. Madeleine loves mending people. She specializes in the mechanical prosthetic, the glass eye, the wooden leg . . . There's nothing you won't find in her workshop.

As this nineteenth century draws to a close, it takes scarcely more to be suspected of witchcraft. In town, people say that Madeleine kills newborns to model slaves from ectoplasm, and that she sleeps with all sorts of birds to conceive monsters.

During her long labor, my mother watches distractedly as snowflakes and birds silently smash their faces against the window. She's very young, like a child playing at being pregnant. Her mood is gloomy; she knows she won't keep me. She can scarcely bring herself to look down at her belly, which is ready to burst. As I threaten to arrive, her eyelids close without tensing. Her skin merges with the sheets: as if the bed is sucking her up, as if she's melting.

She was already weeping on the climb up the hill to get here. Her frozen tears bounced off the ground, like beads from a broken necklace. As she walked, a carpet of glittering ball bearings sprang up under her feet. She began to skate, then found she couldn't stop. The cadence of her steps became too quick. Her heels got caught, her ankles lurched and she went sprawling. Inside her, I made a noise like a broken piggybank.

Dr. Madeleine is my first sighting. Her fingers grab my olive-shaped skull—a miniature rugby ball—and then we snuggle up peacefully.

My mother prefers to look away. In any case, her eyelids no longer want to function. *"Open your eyes! Look at this miniature snowflake you've made!"*

Madeleine says I look like a white bird with big feet. My mother replies that if she's not looking at me, then the last thing she wants is a description.

"I don't want to see, and I don't want to know!"

But the doctor seems preoccupied. She keeps palpating my tiny torso. The smile disappears from her face.

"His heart is very hard. I think it's frozen."

"Mine too. There's no need to make a fuss."

"But his heart really *is* frozen!"

She shakes me from top to bottom, and I make the same noise as someone rummaging in a toolbox.

Dr. Madeleine busies herself in front of her worktop. My mother waits, sitting on her bed. She's trembling now and, this time, it has nothing to do with the cold. She's like a porcelain doll that escaped from the toy shop.

Outside, the snow is falling more thickly. Silver ivy

climbs over the rooftops. Translucent roses bend toward windows, lighting up the streets. Cats become gargoyles, their claws stuck in the gutter.

Fish are pulling faces in the river, frozen midswim. The whole city is in the clutches of a glassblower, who exhales an ear-biting cold. In a matter of seconds, the few brave people who dare to head outside are paralyzed; you'd think some deity had just taken their photograph. Carried along by the momentum of their own scurrying, some start gliding to the rhythm of a final dance. They almost look handsome, each assuming his or her own style, twisted angels with their scarves sticking up in the sky, music-box dancers at the close of their performance, slowing down to the bars of their very last breath.

Everywhere, passers-by already frozen—or on their way to freezing—impale themselves on the rose garden of fountains. Only the clocks continue to make the heart of the city beat, as if none of this were out of the ordinary.

They warned me not to climb to the top of Arthur's Seat. Everyone said the old lady was mad, thinks my mother. The poor girl looks like she's dying of cold. If the doctor manages to mend my own heart, I reckon she'll have an even bigger job with my mother's . . . Here I am, lying stark naked, waiting on the workbench next to the worktop, my chest clamped in a metal vise. And I'm starting to feel seriously cold.

An ancient black cat, with a servile manner, is perched

on a kitchen table. The doctor has made him a pair of glasses. Green frames to match his eyes—stylish. Nonchalantly, he watches the scene, all he's missing is a financial newspaper and a cigar.

Dr. Madeleine starts scouring the shelf of windup clocks. She removes a number of different models: severe-looking angular ones, round ones, wooden ones and metal ones, showing off to the tips of their clock hands. With one ear she listens to my defective heart, with the other to the tick-tocks of the clocks. She scrunches her eyes, apparently unsatisfied. She's like one of those dreadful old ladies who takes a quarter of an hour to choose a tomato at the market. All of a sudden, her face lights up. "This one!" she shrieks, stroking the gears of an old cuckoo clock.

The clock measures approximately four centimeters by eight, and is made entirely from wood with the exception of its mechanical parts, dial and handles. The finish is rather rustic, "sturdy," thinks the doctor out loud. The cuckoo, tall as my little finger bone, is red with black eyes. Its beak, fixed open, gives it the air of a dead bird.

"You'll have a good heart with this clock! And it'll be an excellent match for your birdlike head," Dr. Madeleine says to me.

I'm not so keen on this bird business. That said, she is trying to save my life, so I don't quibble.

Dr. Madeleine puts on a white apron. This time I'm sure she's going to set to work cooking. I feel like the grilled chicken they forgot to kill. She hunts around in a salad bowl, chooses a pair of welder's glasses and covers her face with a handkerchief. I can't see her smiling anymore. She leans over and forces me to breathe in the ether. My eyelids close, surrendering like shutters on a summer's evening somewhere far away from here. I don't want to call out anymore. I watch her, then sleep slowly overcomes me. Everything about her is curved: her eyes, her cheeks like russet apples, her bosom. She's made for wrapping around you. I'll pretend to be hungry even when I'm not, just to tuck into her breasts.

Madeleine snips through the skin on my chest using a large pair of scissors with serrated edges. The touch of their little teeth tickles. She slides the clock under my skin and begins to connect the gears to the arteries of my heart. It's a delicate process; nothing can afford to be damaged. She uses an ultrafine, solid steel wire to make a dozen miniature knots. The heart beats from time to time, but only a feeble quantity of blood is pumped into the arteries. "How white he is!" she whispers.

It's the hour of truth. Dr. Madeleine sets the clock to dead on midnight . . . Nothing happens. The clockwork apparatus doesn't seem powerful enough to stimulate the heart. I've had no heartbeat for a dangerously long time. My head is spinning, in an exhausting dream. The doctor presses down gently on the gears to set things in motion. *Tick-tock,* goes the clock. *Bo-boom,* the heart replies, and the arteries run red. Little by little, the tick-tock gets faster, and so too does the bo-boom. Tick-tock. Bo-boom. Tick-tock. Bo-boom. My heart is almost beating at normal speed. Dr. Madeleine gently removes her fingers from the gears. The clock slows down. She restarts the device; but as soon as she takes her fingers away, the heartbeat grows weaker. She's like someone cuddling a bomb, wondering when it'll explode.

Tick-tock. Bo-boom. Tick-tock. Bo-boom.

The first rays of light bounce off the snow and sneak in through the shutters. Dr. Madeleine is exhausted. As for me, I've fallen asleep; perhaps I'm dead, because my heart stopped for too long.

Just then, a cuckoo sings so loudly in my chest that I cough in surprise. Eyes wide open, I spot Dr. Madeleine with her arms in the air, like she's just scored a penalty in a World Cup final.

She starts stitching my chest with the skill of an accomplished tailor; I'm not exactly battered but my skin looks old, with wrinkles like Charles Bronson. Stylish. The dial is protected by an enormous bandage.

Every morning, I need to be wound up with the key. Otherwise I risk drifting off to sleep forever.

My mother says I look like a big snowflake with clock hands sticking out. Madeleine replies that it's a good system for finding me again in a snowstorm.

It is midday and the doctor, with her warm habit of smiling in the midst of catastrophes, escorts this wisp of a girl to the door. My young mother walks slowly. Her lips tremble.

Off she heads into the distance, a dejected old woman in the body of a teenager. As she merges with the mist, she becomes a porcelain ghost. I will never set eyes on her again after this strange and miraculous day.

chapter two

Makeshift hearts, rusty spines, and a trip to the ground floor of the mountain

Every day, Madeleine has visitors knocking on her door. Patients end up here when they've broken something but can't afford a "qualified" doctor. Whether she's fine-tuning, or mending and discussing, Madeleine likes tinkering with people's hearts. I don't feel such an oddity with my clockwork heart when I hear a client complaining about his rusty spine.

"It's made of metal, what did you expect?"

"Yes, but it creaks when I move my arm!"

"I've already prescribed an umbrella for you. I know it can be hard to find one at the pharmacy. I'll lend you mine this time, but try to get hold of one before our next meeting."

I am also witness to the parade of young, well-dressed couples who climb the hill to adopt the children they haven't managed to have themselves. It's rather like a house-viewing. Madeleine sings the praises of this or that child who never cries, eats a balanced diet and is already potty trained.

Made to sit on a sofa, I await my turn. I'm the smallest model; you could almost squeeze me into a sock box. When the prospective parents turn their attention to me, they always start off with fake smiles, until one of them pipes up: "Where is that *tick-tock-tick-tock* coming from?"

At which point the doctor sits me on her knee, unbuttons my clothes and reveals my bandage. Some shriek, others just make a face and say:

"Oh my God! What on earth *is* that thing?"

"If it had been up to God, we wouldn't be talking now. This *'thing,'* as you call it, is a clock that allows this child's heart to beat normally," she answers drily.

The young couples look embarrassed and go off to whisper in the next room, but the verdict is always the same:

"No, thank you. Could we see some other children?"

"Yes, follow me, I have two little girls who were born during Christmas week," she suggests, brightly.

. . .

At first, I didn't understand what was going on. I was too young. But as I've grown older, I've become frustrated with my role as the mongrel of the kennel. How can a simple clock put people off me so badly? It's only wood, after all.

Today, after I've failed to be adopted for the umpteenth time, one of the doctor's regular patients approaches me. Arthur is an ex–police officer turned alcoholic tramp. Everything about him is crumpled, from his overcoat to his eyelids. He's quite tall. He'd be even taller if he stood up straight. He doesn't usually speak to me. And curious as it may sound, I enjoy our habit of not talking. There's something reassuring about the way he limps across the kitchen, half smiling and waving his hand.

While Madeleine is looking after the young, well-dressed couples in the adjacent room, Arthur waddles around. His spine creaks like a prison gate. Finally, he says, in his thick Scottish brogue:

"Don't worry, little one! Nothing lasts forever. We always get better in the end, even if it takes time. I lost my job a few weeks before the coldest day on earth, and my wife kicked me out. To think I agreed to join the police just for her. I used to dream about becoming a musician, but we were painfully short of money."

"What happened to make the police want to get rid of you?"

"A leopard doesn't change his spots! I used to sing the

witness statements instead of reading them aloud, and I spent more time on my harmonium than on the police station typewriter. Plus I drank the odd drop of whisky; just enough to give me a husky voice . . . But they had no appreciation, you see? In the end, they asked me to leave. That was when I had the unfortunate task of explaining things to my wife. You know the rest. So I spent what little money I had left on whisky. That's what saved my life, you know."

I love his habit of saying "you know." Solemnly, he explains to me how whisky "saved his life."

"On that notorious day of April 16, 1874, the cold cracked my spine: the only thing that prevented me from freezing altogether was the warmth from the alcohol I'd forced down, following those dark events. I'm the only tramp who survived. All my cronies froze to death."

He takes off his coat and asks me to take a look at his back. It's embarrassing, but I can't say no.

"To mend the broken section, Dr. Madeleine grafted on bits of musical spine and then tuned its bones. So I can play different tunes if I hit my back with a hammer. It sounds nice, but I do walk sideways like a crab. Go on, play something if you'd like," he says, holding out his little hammer.

"I don't know how to play anything!"

"Hold on, hold on, we'll sing together, you'll see."

He starts singing "When the Saints Go Marching In," accompanying himself with his bone-o-phone. His voice is as comforting as a crackling fire in hearth on a winter's evening.

When he leaves, he opens up his pouch, which is full of hen's eggs.

"Why are you carrying all those eggs around?"

"Because they're full of memories . . . My wife used to cook them wonderfully. When I cook them just for me, I feel like I'm back with her again."

"Can you cook them as well as she did?"

"No, they always turn out nasty, but at least it's easier for me keep our memories alive. Take one, if you like."

"I don't want you to be missing a memory."

"Oh, don't worry, pet. I've got plenty. You won't appreciate this yet, but one day you'll be happy to open your bag and find a memory from your childhood in there."

For the time being, as soon as the minor chords of "When the Saints Go Marching In" start to play, my worries fade away for a few hours.

After my fifth birthday, the doctor stops showing me to her customers, the prospective parents. There are more and more questions in my head, and every day the need for answers grows stronger.

My desire to discover the "ground floor of the mountain" becomes an obsession. I notice a mysterious rumbling when I climb up onto the roof, alone with the night.

The moonlight tinges the streets of the town center with a sugary halo, which I dream of tasting.

Madeleine keeps on reminding me that there will be time to confront the reality of the city soon enough.

"Each beat of your heart is a small miracle, you know, so don't get carried away. It's a fragile, makeshift repair. Things should get better as you grow up, but you'll have to be patient."

"How many times will the big hand have to go round?"

"A few . . . a few. I want your heart to become a bit more robust before I let you out into nature."

There's no denying that my clock causes me a worry or two. It's the most sensitive part of my body. I can't bear anyone to touch it, apart from Madeleine. She winds me up every morning using a small key. When I catch a cold, the coughing hurts my gears. It feels as if they're about to poke out through my skin. And I hate that sound of broken crockery they make.

But mostly I'm worried about being always out of kilter. By evening, the *tick-tock* that reverberates through my body stops me from sleeping. I might collapse with exhaustion in the middle of the afternoon, but I feel on top of the world in the dead of night. I'm not a hamster or a vampire, just an insomniac.

Then again, as is often the case with people who suffer from an illness, there are a few advantages. I love those precious moments when Madeleine glides into my bedroom like a ghost in her nightgown, a cup of hot chocolate in her hand, to calm my insomnia with haunting lullabies.

Sometimes she sings until dawn, caressing my gears with her fingertips. It's a tender moment. *Love is dangerous for your tiny heart,* she repeats hypnotically. She could be chanting from an old book of magic spells, to help me get to sleep. I like to hear her voice ringing out under a star-filled sky, even if there's something strange about the way she whispers *love is dangerous for your tiny heart.*

On my tenth birthday, Dr. Madeleine finally agrees to take me into town. I've been pleading with her for such a long time . . . Even so, right up until the last moment, she can't help trying to postpone the big event, tidying things instead, walking from one room to another.

While I'm down in the cellar, stamping my feet impatiently, I discover a shelf lined with jars. Some are labelled *"Tears 1850–1857,"* and others are filled with *"Apples from the Garden."*

"Who do all those tears belong to?" I ask her.

"They're mine. Whenever I start crying, I collect my tears in a flask and store them in the cellar to make cocktails."

"How did you manage to shed so many tears?"

"When I was young, an embryo got lost on its way to my womb. It became stuck in one of my tubes, causing me to bleed inside. Ever since that day, I've been unable to have children. I cried a lot, even though I'm happy to bring other people's children into the world. But things are better now that you're here . . ."

I'm ashamed I even asked her.

"After one particular day of sobbing, I noticed the tears were comforting to drink, especially when mixed with cider vinegar. But you mustn't drink when you're feeling fine, otherwise you're caught in a vicious circle of only feeling happy when drinking your own tears, so you have to keep on crying in order to drink."

"But you spend your time mending other people, so why drown your wounds in the alcohol of your own tears?"

"Let's not worry about all that, we're heading down into town today! Haven't we got a birthday to celebrate?" she asks, forcing a smile.

After the disturbing story of Madeleine's tears, it takes a while for me to feel excited as we head down the hill. But as soon as I see Edinburgh, my dreams get the upper hand.

I feel like Christopher Columbus discovering America. The twisted maze of streets beckons like a lover. Houses lean toward each other, shrinking the sky. I'm running! A single breath could bring the whole city tumbling down in a game of brick dominoes. I'm running! The trees are still stuck up there on top of the hill, but down here people are springing up everywhere, the women an explosion of flowers, poppy-hats, poppy-dresses. I see them leaning out of balcony windows, as far as the market that brightens Salisbury Place.

I'm taking it all in: clogs ringing out over the cobble-stones, mingled voices that carry me away. And the great bell tower, tolling with a heart ten times bigger than mine.

"Is that my father?"

"No, no, it's not your father . . . It's chiming for one o'clock, it only tolls once a day," Madeleine answers, out of breath.

We cross the square. Music can be heard round the corner of a side street, as mischievous and melancholic as harmonious glitter. The melody takes my breath away; inside me, it's raining and shining at the same time.

"That's a barrel organ. Nice, isn't it?" Madeleine tells me. "It functions in much the same way as your heart, which is probably why you like it so much. It's mechanical on the outside, with emotions on the inside."

I'm convinced I've just heard the most delightful sound of my life, but the fiery surprises have only just begun. A minuscule girl, like a tree in blossom, steps out in front of the barrel organ and begins to sing. Her voice is like a nightingale's, but with words.

"My spectacles have been mislaid
I didn't want to wear 'em
Fire-girl behind those shades
My face looked funny, I'm afraid."

Her arms look like branches and her curly black hair sets her face aglow, playing the shadow to its fire. Her tiny nose is so perfect, I don't know how she can breathe through it—perhaps it's just for decoration. But she dances like a bird, on the feminine scaffolding of stiletto heels. Her eyes are so huge that you can take your time plunging in. They betray a fierce determination. She carries her head high, like a miniature flamenco dancer. Her breasts resemble two meringues so exquisitely baked it would be rude not to eat them on the spot.

"I don't mind if I'm half blind
When I sing or when I kiss,
I prefer to close my eyes
In this hazy state of bliss."

I feel hot. The little singer's merry-go-round terrifies me, but I'm also dying to climb up there. The smell of candyfloss and dust makes my throat feel parched. I've got no idea how this pink carousel works, but I have to climb on board.

Suddenly, just like in a musical comedy, I burst into song. Dr. Madeleine gives me a look that says "take your hands off that stove now."

"Oh my little fire, let me taste your attire,
Shred your clothes to a tatter,
As confetti make them scatter,
Then I'll kiss you in that shower . . ."

Did I hear myself say "confetti"? Madeleine's gaze speaks volumes.

"Lost in a heartbeat,
Far away on my own street,

Can't look the sky in the eye,
All I see is fire."

We began to sing together, back and forth.

"I'll guide you through this city's passes,
And be your special pair of glasses,
You'll be the match I strike,
Yes, you'll be the match I strike."

"I've got something to admit,
I hear you now but should you sit
Upon a bench, I couldn't tell
Between your handsome self and it!" ·

"Let's stroke each other, eyes shut tight,
'Til our skeletons catch alight,
Let's start a fire on the hour
My cuckoo-clock chimes midnight."

"I'm a little fire-girl, so it's no surprise
When the music stops I can't open my eyes.
I blaze like a match, a thousand flames burn my glasses,
So it's no surprise, I can't open my eyes."

As our voices rise in unison, her left heel gets caught
between two cobblestones, she teeters like a spinning top
at the end of its flight and lands spread-eagled on the icy

path. An accident of comical violence. Blood runs down her dress in feathers and she looks like a crushed gull. Sprawled on the cobblestones, she still stirs me. She struggles to put on a pair of spectacles with wonky sides, then staggers like a sleepwalker. Her mother holds her more firmly by the hand than is usual for a parent; you could say she's restraining her.

I try to say something, but the words stick in my throat. I wonder how eyes as huge and wonderful as hers can be so ineffectual that she bumps into things.

Dr. Madeleine and the little girl's mother exchange a few words, like the owners of two dogs who've just been in a fight.

My heart races again, I'm finding it hard to catch my breath. Is my clock swelling and rising up in my throat? Has this fire-girl just stepped out of an egg? Is she edible? Is she made of chocolate? What the hell is going on?

I try to look her in the eye, but her mouth has kidnapped my gaze. I didn't know it was possible to spend so much time staring at a mouth.

All of a sudden, my cuckoo-clock heart starts ringing loudly, far louder than when I'm having an attack. I can feel my gears whirring at top speed, as if I've swallowed a helicopter. The chiming hurts my eardrums so I block my ears, which only makes it worse. My clock hands are going to sever my throat. Dr. Madeleine moves to calm me with slow hand gestures, like a bird tamer trying to catch a panicked canary in its cage. I'm horribly hot.

I'd like to be a golden eagle, or a majestically cool sea-gull. But instead I'm a stressed canary ensnared by its own startled movements. I hope the little singer hasn't seen me. My *tick-tock* sounds dull. My eyes open and I'm this close to the blue sky. The doctor's iron fist has clamped down on my shirt collar, gently raising my heels off the ground. Next, Madeleine grabs me by the arm.

"We're going back home, immediately! You've frightened everybody! Everybody!"

She looks furious and worried at the same time. I feel ashamed. But I'm also busy committing to memory the pictures I have of this tiny shrub of a girl, who sings without glasses and stares the sun in the face. Almost without realizing it, I'm falling in love. Except I do realize it too. Inside my clock, it's the hottest day on earth.

After a quarter of an hour of clock maintenance and a delicious bowl of noodle soup, I'm back to my funny old normal state.

Madeleine looks strained, the way she does when she has to sing for too long to get me to sleep, but this time she seems more worried.

"Your heart is only an implant. It's more fragile than a normal heart and it will always be that way. A clockwork mechanism can't filter emotions as well as human tissue. You have to be very careful. What happened in town today when you saw that little singer only confirms my fears: love is too dangerous for you."

"I couldn't take my eyes off her mouth."

"Don't say that!"

"Her dimples are a never-ending game, her smile is always changing, I could watch her forever."

"You don't understand, you think it's a game, but you're playing with fire and that's very dangerous when you have a heart made of wood. Your gears hurt when you cough, don't they?"

"Yes."

"Well, that's nothing compared to the suffering that love can inflict. All love's pleasures and joys are paid for one day with suffering. And the more passionately you love, the more your pain will increase. You'll find out what it means to miss somebody, the torment of jealousy and incomprehension, what it feels like to be rejected and unfairly treated. You'll be chilled to the bone, and your blood will form little blocks of ice that float underneath your skin. Your cuckoo-clock heart will explode. I was the one who grafted that clock on to you, and I have a perfect understanding of its limits. It might survive the intensity of pleasure, and beyond. But it is not robust enough to endure the torment of love."

Madeleine smiles sadly—still that twitch that vanishes instantly, but at least she's not angry this time.

chapter three

In which Little Jack befriends Anna, Luna, and a hamster called Cunnilingus

The mystery surrounding the little singer tantalizes me. In my mind's eye, I stockpile images of her long eyelashes, her dimples, her perfect nose and the curve of her lips. I nurture her memory the way you'd tend a delicate flower. This fills my days.

I can only think of one thing: finding her again. I want to taste that sensation I can't put into words, preferably as soon as possible. So what if the cuckoo risks being spat out through my nose? So what if my heart needs mending more often? I've been having it repaired ever since I was born. So what if I'm in danger of dying? My life's in danger if I don't see her again and, at my age, that's even more serious.

I'm beginning to understand why the doctor was so keen to put off my encounter with the outside world. You only ask for strawberries with sugar every day once you've discovered a taste for them.

Some evenings, the little singer pays me a visit in my dreams. Tonight, she's two centimeters tall. She enters my heart through its keyhole and straddles my hour hand. She fixes me with her elegant doelike eyes. I may be asleep, but it's still an impressive sight. Gently, she starts licking my minute hand. She's gathering my nectar; something clockwork starts whirring into action, and I'm not sure it's just my heart . . . TICK-TOCK DING! TICK-TOCK DONG! Bloody cuckoo! I wake up with a jolt.

"Love is dangerous for your tiny heart, even in your dreams, so please dream softly," Madeleine whispers to me. "Go back to sleep . . ."

As if that was easy with a heart like mine.

The next day, I'm woken by the tapping of a hammer. Madeleine is standing on a chair, banging a nail into the wall above my bed. She looks very determined, and she's got a piece of slate between her teeth. She might as well be driving a nail straight into my skull. Then she hangs up the slate, which has the following words inscribed sinisterly upon it:

FIRSTLY: DON'T TOUCH THE HANDS OF YOUR CUCKOO-CLOCK HEART. SECONDLY: MASTER YOUR ANGER. THIRDLY: NEVER, EVER FALL IN LOVE. FOR IF YOU DO, THE HOUR HAND WILL POKE THROUGH YOUR SKIN, YOUR BONES WILL SHATTER, AND YOUR HEART WILL BREAK ONCE MORE.

The slate terrorizes me. I don't even need to read what's on it, I know the words inside out and back to front. And they blow an ill wind between my gears.

But fragile as my clock may be, the little singer has settled in comfortably. She's set down her heavy suitcases in every corner, and yet I'm lighter than before I met her.

It doesn't matter what it costs, I have to find a way of tracking her down again. What's her name? Where can I find her? I know she can't see very well and sings like a bird, but with words. That's all.

I try discreetly asking the young couples who come to Dr. Madeleine's to adopt. No answer. I hazard my luck with Arthur. "I heard her singing in town once, but I haven't seen her for a while now, pet." The girls might be more inclined to point me in the right direction.

Anna and Luna are two prostitutes who always turn up around Christmas time with downcast looks at their rounded tummies. From the way they keep saying: "No, no, we don't know anything, absolutely nothing . . . nothing at all, do we Anna? Not a single thing, not us," I can tell I'm on the right track.

They look like two overgrown kids. Which is what they are, two thirty-year-old kids, with clingy leopard-skin costumes. Their clothes always have a strange whiff of Provençal herbs, even when they're not smoking. Their cigarettes create a foggy halo and make the girls laugh so hard they must be getting their brains tickled. Their favorite game involves teaching me new words. They never reveal the meanings, they just want to make sure I can pronounce everything perfectly. Of all the wonderful names they teach me, my favorite is *cunnilingus.* I imagine him as an ancient Roman hero, this Cunnilingus. You have to say it again and again, Cun-ni-lin-gus, Cunnilingus, Cunnilingus. What a fantastic word!

Anna and Luna never show up empty-handed. There's always a bunch of flowers nicked from the cemetery, or the frock coat of a client who croaked during coitus. For my birthday, they gave me a hamster. I called it Cunnilingus. They seemed very touched that I chose that name. "Cunnilingus, my love!" Luna always sings to it, as she taps the bars of its cage with her painted nails.

Anna is a tall faded rose with a rainbow gaze; her left pupil is a quartz stone, inserted by Madeleine to replace the eye that was gouged out by a customer who didn't want to pay, and it changes color with the weather. She speaks quickly, like she's scared of silence. When I ask her about the little singer, she tells me she's *never heard of her.* But her words come out even faster than usual. I can tell she's dying to let me in on a great secret so I decide to ask her a question or two about love, but in hushed tones, because I don't really want Madeleine meddling.

"I've been working at love for a long time, you know. I haven't always been on the receiving end of a great deal of it, but sometimes just the simple act of giving makes me happy. I'm no good as a professional. I fall in love as soon as someone's a regular customer; then I start refusing their money. For a while they come every day, and even bring me presents. But their enthusiasm wears off eventually. I know I'm not supposed to fall for them, I just can't help it. It's ridiculous, but I enjoy believing in the impossible."

"The impossible?"

"It's not easy being simple-hearted when you're in my profession."

"I think I understand."

And then there's Luna, a shimmering blonde, a forerunner of the famous Egyptian singer Dalida, with her slow gestures and broken smile, a tightrope walker on the most spindly stilettos. Part of her right leg froze on the coldest day on earth. Madeleine replaced it with a walnut wood prosthesis complete with its own pokerwork suspender. She reminds me of the little singing girl—they share the same nightingale accent, the same spontaneity.

"You wouldn't happen to know a little singer who talks just like you and who's always bumping into things?" I ask her every now and then.

She pretends not to hear me and changes the subject. I

suppose Madeleine's made them promise not to let on about the little singer.

One fine day, bored with ignoring my litany of questions, she replies:

"I don't know anything about the little Andalusian . . ."

"What's an *Andalusian*?"

"I didn't say anything, nothing at all! Why don't you ask Anna?"

"Anna doesn't know anything either . . ."

I try the old trick of sad boy, head down, eyes half closed.

"From what I can see, you've already learned the basics of seduction," Anna continues. "Do you promise not to tell anee-bodd-ee?"

"Of course not!"

She starts whispering, and her words are barely audible:

"Your little singer comes from Granada, in Andalusia, which is far away from here. It's been a long time since I heard her singing in town . . . Perhaps she's gone back to the country where she was born, to live with her grandparents . . ."

"Unless she's just at school," adds Anna, her voice like a 33 r.p.m. record being played at 45 r.p.m.

"Thank you!"

"Ssssh . . . *¡cállate!*" snaps Luna, who only breaks into her native tongue when she's annoyed.

My blood's fizzing, I can't believe my luck. A surge of pure joy. My dream puffs up like a pastry in the oven. I think it's ready to make the journey into reality now. Tomorrow, I'll harness my energy at the top of the hill, unfurl my mainsail, and head for the school!

Except that first, I'll have to convince Madeleine.

"Go to school? But you'll get bored! You'll be forced to read books you don't like, when here you can choose whatever takes your fancy. You'll have to sit for hours on end and you won't be allowed to talk, or make a noise. You'll be made to wait until break time just to daydream. I know what you're like—how much you'll hate it."

"Perhaps, but I'm curious to find out what people learn at school."

"You want to study?"

"Yes, that's right. I want to study. And I can't do it all on my own here."

We're trying to outmaneuver each other with our lies. I'm caught between wanting to laugh and flying into a rage.

"To start with, you'd be better off reviewing what's written on your slate. It seems to me you're forgetting it rather too quickly. I worry about what might happen to you down there."

"Everybody goes to school. When you're at work, I feel all alone on top of this mountain, and I'd like to meet some children my own age. It's time for me to find out about the world, don't you see?"

"Finding out about the world at school . . ." (A long sigh.)

"All right. If you want to go to school, I won't stand in your way," Madeleine eventually concedes, sounding as if a small part of her has died.

I try my best to contain my joy. It might not be very tactful to dance around with my arms in the air.

The day I've been waiting for has come at last. I'm wearing a black suit that makes me look very grown-up, in spite of my eleven years. Madeleine has instructed me never to take off my jacket, not even in class; that way nobody will find out about my cuckoo clock.

Before setting off, I'm careful to slip a few pairs of glasses that I've collected from her workshop into my satchel. They take up more room than the exercise books. I've moved Cunnilingus into my left shirt pocket, just above my clockwork heart. He pokes his head out from time to time, looking thoroughly satisfied.

"Be careful he doesn't bite anybody!" joke Anna and Luna, as we start down the hill.

Limping some way behind us comes Arthur, creaking silently.

The school is located in the well-heeled area of Calton Hill, just opposite St. Giles's Cathedral. Over by the entrance, it's a country of fur coats and women cackling loudly as big hens. The way Anna and Luna laugh makes them scowl. They observe Arthur's limping gait and the bump that makes my left lung swell suspiciously. Their husbands, suited and booted, look like walking coat hangers; they pretend to be shocked by our twisted tribe, but that doesn't stop them from eyeballing the two girls' cleavages.

After a quick goodbye to my makeshift family, I walk through the huge gates—you'd think I'd been enrolled in an institution for giants. The schoolyard looks impossible to cross, even if its football goalposts add a slightly welcoming touch.

I take my first tentative steps, scrutinizing the different faces. The pupils look like miniature versions of their parents. My clock can be heard rather too clearly through their whispering. They're looking at me as if I've got an infectious disease. All of a sudden, a brown-haired girl stands in front of me, stares, and starts saying "tick-tock, tick-tock" and laughing. The whole yard joins in. It feels just the same as when families come to Dr. Madeleine's to choose their children—but worse. Even though I examine every girl's face, there is no sign of the little singer. What if Luna made a mistake?

We go into the classroom. Madeleine was right, I'm bored rigid. Bloody school without the little singer . . . and now I'm enrolled for the whole year. How am I going to tell Madeleine I don't want to "study" now?

During break I begin my survey by asking if anybody knows the little "Andalusian" singer, the one who's always bumping into things.

Nobody answers.

"Doesn't she go to school here?"

No answer.

I wonder if anything serious has happened to her. Did she bump into something hard and hurt herself badly?

Just then, an odd-looking boy rises up from the ranks. He's older than the others, and the top of his head is almost higher than the railings. The moment they see him, the rest of the students cower. His jet-black eyes make my blood run cold. He's skinny as a dead tree, elegant as a scarecrow dressed by a fine tailor, and his spiky hair juts out like birds' wings.

"Hey you! New boy! What d'you want with the little singer?"

His voice is deep as a talking tombstone.

"One day, I saw her singing and bumping into things. I'd like to give her a pair of glasses as a present."

My voice is quavering. I must look at least a hundred and thirty.

"Nobody's allowed to talk to me about Miss Acacia and her spectacles! Nobody, you understand, least of all a midget like you. Don't ever mention her name again. D'you understand, midget?"

I don't answer. A murmur rises from the crowd: "Joe . . ." Each second weighs heavily. Suddenly, he cocks his ear in my direction and asks:

"How do you make that strange tick-tock noise?"

I don't say anything.

He heads calmly over to me, stooping his tall carcass to put his ear next to my heart. My clock is palpitating. Time has stopped for me. His boy's beard stings like barbed wire across my chest. Cunnilingus points his snout and sniffs the top of Joe's head. If he starts peeing, things could get complicated.

All of a sudden, Joe tears off my buttons and rips open my jacket to expose the clock hands poking out of my shirt. The crowd of curious onlookers goes "Ooooh . . ." I'm so embarrassed, he might as well have pulled my trousers down. He listens to my heart for a while, then stands up slowly.

"Is that your heart making all that noise?"

"Yes."

"You're in love with her, aren't you?"

His deep, conceited voice makes all my bones shiver.

My brain wants to say *no, no* . . . but my heart has faster access to my lips.

"Yes, I am."

The students start whispering *"Ooohh . . ."* The anger blazing at the back of Joe's eyes is tinged with sadness, which makes him even more terrifying. Just one look from him and the schoolyard falls silent. Even the wind seems to obey him.

"The 'little singer,' as you call her, is the love of my life and . . . she's not here anymore. Don't you ever dare talk to me about her again! I don't even want to hear you thinking about her, or I'll smash that wooden clock over your head. I'll break it, do you hear me? I'll break it so badly, you'll NEVER be able to love again!"

His long fingers quiver with rage, even when he clenches his fist.

Just a few hours ago, I thought my heart was a ship ready to cut through an ocean of disapproval. I knew it wasn't the sturdiest heart in the world, but I believed in the strength of my own enthusiasm. I was so fired up by the idea of finding the little singer that nothing could have stopped me. In less than five minutes, Joe has reset my clock to real time, swapping my colorful galleon for a dilapidated old tub.

"I'll break it so badly, you'll NEVER be able to love again!" he says one more time.

"Cuckoo," answers my wooden hull.

The sound of my own voice is cut short; you'd think I'd just been punched in the gut.

As I climb back up Arthur's Seat, I wonder how such a gorgeous bespectacled goldfinch could have fallen into the claws of a vulture like Joe. I try to cheer myself with the thought that perhaps my little singer came to school without her glasses on and that she couldn't see what she was getting herself into . . . Where could she be now?

A middle-aged woman interrupts my anxious reverie. She's holding Joe firmly by the hand—unless it's the other way round, given the vulture's size. She looks like him, just a more withered version, and with an elephant's arse.

"Are you the boy who lives up there with the witch? Did you know she delivers children from prostitutes' bellies? You probably came out of a prostitute's belly too, everyone knows the old lady's been barren for a long time."

When adults get involved, a new threshold of ugliness is always crossed.

Despite my obstinate silence, Joe and his mother carry on insulting me for a good part of the journey. I struggle to reach the top of the hill. The day weighs so heavily on my clock hands that I'm having to drag myself along like a ball and chain. Bloody clock of dreams! I'd happily hurl you down Arthur's Seat.

That evening, no matter how much Madeleine sings to help send me off to sleep, it doesn't work. When I decide to tell her about Joe, she explains that perhaps he treated me like that to look big in other people's eyes, and that he's not necessarily all bad. He must be very smitten with the little singer too. The torment of love can transform people into wretched monsters, she tells me. It annoys me that she's making excuses for him. She kisses me on my clock dial and slows down my cardiac rate by pressing on my gears with her index finger. I close my eyes in the end, but I'm not smiling.

chapter four

A fistful of emotions, a poked-out eye, and a hasty departure from Edinburgh

A year goes by, with Joe sticking to me as if magnetized by my clock hands, punching my clock in full view of everybody. Sometimes I want to tear out his crow-black shock of hair; I try not to flinch when he humiliates me, but he's getting me down. My quest to find the little singer is proving fruitless. Nobody dares answer my questions. At school, Joe is the law.

Today, at break, I take out Arthur's egg from one of my pullover sleeves. I'm trying to track down Miss Acacia by thinking about her as hard as I can. I forget about Joe, I even forget I'm in this bloody school. As I stroke the egg, a beautiful dream glides across the screen of my eyelids. The eggshell cracks open and the little singer appears, her body covered in red feathers. I hold her between my thumb and index finger, frightened of crushing her but not wanting her to fly away. A tender fire sparks between my fingers and her eyes flicker open, when all of a sudden my skull goes "crack!"

Egg yolk is trickling down my cheeks—the tears of my dream draining away. Joe towers over the scene with the remains of eggshell between his fingers. Everybody's laughing and some people even applaud.

"Next time, I'll smash your heart against your skull."

In class, everyone makes fun of the eggshell pieces stuck in my hair. I'm itching for revenge. The fairies in my dreams vanish. I spend nearly as much time despising Joe as I do loving Miss Acacia. Dreams have a hard time surviving when confronted with reality.

Joe's humiliations continue day after day. I've become the toy that he uses to calm his nerves and dull his melancholy. No matter how often I water the flowers that are my memories of the little singer, they're being starved of sunlight.

Madeleine goes to great lengths to comfort me, but she never wants to hear any tales of the heart. Arthur hardly has any memory eggs left in his pouch, and he sings less and less.

On my birthday, Anna and Luna come over for the

evening—it's the same "surprise" every year. As usual, they're having fun putting perfume on Cunnilingus, but this time Luna gets a little overenthusiastic when she douses him. The hamster stiffens in a spasm and keels over, stone dead. The sight of my faithful companion stretched out in his cage makes me very sad. A long "cuckoo" escapes from my chest.

As a consolation prize, I get a geography lesson on Andalusia from Luna. Ah, *Andalusia* . . . If only I could be sure that Miss Acacia was there, I'd leave right away!

Four years have gone by since my encounter with the little singer, and nearly three years since I started school. I still look for her everywhere, but I can never find her. Little by little, my memories are being crushed under the weight of time.

On the night before the last day of school, I go to bed with a bitter aftertaste in my mouth. I don't get a wink of sleep. I'm too busy thinking about what I want to achieve tomorrow. Because this time I've made up my mind, it's time to conquer the Amorous West. I just need to find out where the little singer is right now. And the only person who can answer that question is Joe. I watch dawn tracing the shadows to the beat of my *tick-tock*.

It's June 27 and we're in the school playground under a blue sky, so blue you'd think we were anywhere but Edinburgh. The sleepless night has sharpened my nerves.

I make straight for Joe, with more than purpose in my

stride. But before I've had a chance to say anything, he grabs my shirt collar and hoicks me off the ground. My heart creaks, my anger overflows, the cuckoo hisses. Joe taunts the crowd around us.

"Take off your shirt and show us what you've got on your chest. We want to see your thing that goes tick-tock."

"Yeah!!!" roars the crowd.

With a swoop of his arm, he rips off my shirt and jams his nails into my dial.

"How does this open?"

"You need a key."

"Hand it over."

"I haven't got it here, it's at home, so leave me alone."

He picks the lock with his little finger, niggling at it furiously. The dial gives way in the end.

"See, we don't need a key after all! Who wants to have a grope?"

One after another, students who've never said a word to me take it in turns to tug on my clock hands and activate my gears. They're hurting me and they're not even looking at me. The cuckoo can't stop hiccuping. They clap and laugh. The whole playground joins in: *"Cuckoo-cuckoo-cuckoo-cuckoo!"*

Something flips inside my brain. Dreams anesthetized for years, pent-up rage, humiliation . . . everything is headed for the floodgates. The barrage is about to give way. I can't hold back any more.

"Where's Miss Acacia?"

"I don't think I heard you properly," says Joe, twisting my arm.

"Where is she? Tell me where she is. I'll find her, whether she's here or in Andalusia, do you hear me?"

Joe pins me face down to the ground, so I can't move. My cuckoo is singing at the top of its voice, I feel like my esophagus is on fire, something's changing inside me. Violent spasms shake me every three seconds. Joe turns around triumphantly.

"So, you're setting off for Andalusia just like that?" he asks, through gritted teeth.

"Yes, I'm leaving! And I'm leaving today!"

My eyes are bulging, so is my throat, and my movements too. I'm turning into a pair of shears that will chop up anyone and anything.

Pretending to be a dog sniffing a turd, Joe brings his nose close to my clock. The whole playground bursts out laughing. This is too much. I grab him by the neck and ram his face against my clock hands. His skull cracks loudly against my wooden heart. The clapping stops dead. I deal him a second blow, more violent this time, then a third. Time seems to stand still. I'd love a photograph to document this moment. His first cries for help shatter the silence, just as the first spurts of blood splatter the nicely ironed clothes of the creeps in the front row. When the hour hand impales itself on the pupil of his right eye, his socket turns into a bloody fountain. All Joe's terror is concentrated in his left eye, as it watches the shower of his own blood. I relax my grip and Joe yelps like a poodle whose paw has accidentally been trodden on. The blood trickles between his fingers. I don't feel the slightest bit of compassion for him. Silence follows, and it lasts.

My clock's burning. I can barely touch it. Joe doesn't move. Is he dead? I'd like him to stop wiping his feet on my dreams, but I don't necessarily want him dead. I'm starting to feel frightened now. The sky shimmers with beads of blood. All around us, kids stand like statues. Perhaps I really have killed Joe. Who'd have thought that one day I'd be worried about Joe dying.

I run away, the whole world on my heels as I cross the playground. I climb up the left pillar and clamber onto the school roof. The realization of what I've just done chills me to the bone. My heart produces the same noise as when I first fell in love with the little singer. Up on the roof, I can make out the top of Arthur's Seat goring the mist. *Oh Madeleine, how furious you'd be . . .*

A swarm of migrating birds hovers above me, as if stacked on a bank of clouds. I'd like to catch hold of their wings and tear myself away from the earth; if only my heart's troubles would take flight, nothing else would matter. Please, dear birds, take me to Andalusia, and I'll find my way from there.

But the birds are out of reach, like chocolate piled high on a shelf, or the alcoholic flasks of tears in the cellar, or my dream of the little singer where I have to climb over

Joe in order to get to her. If I've killed him, things will be even more complicated. My clock is throbbing. Madeleine, you've got your work cut out.

I must try to turn back time. I grab the hour hand that's still warm with blood, and tug it backward in one quick stroke.

My gears whine, the pain is unbearable. Nothing happens. I hear shouting, they're heading this way from the playground. Joe is holding his right eye. I'm almost reassured to hear the injured poodle yelping.

A teacher intervenes and I hear the children denouncing me, all eyes scouring the playground like radar. Panicked, I tumble from the roof and jump into the first tree I see. I scratch my arms on the branches and go crashing to the ground. Adrenaline gives me wings. My legs have never been in such a hurry to get to the top of the mountain.

"Did you have a nice day at school today?" Madeleine asks, as she tidies her shopping away into the kitchen cupboard.

"Yes and no," I answer, trembling all over.

She looks at me, sees my twisted hour hand, and fixes me with a disapproving stare.

"You saw the little singer again, didn't you? The last time you came home with your heart in such a filthy mess, you'd heard her singing."

Madeleine talks to me like I'm a schoolboy sloping home with his best shoes ruined after playing football.

As she tries to straighten my clock hand with a crowbar, I start telling her about the fight. But it makes my heart beat faster again.

"You've been very foolish!"

"Can I turn back time by making my clock hands go backward?"

"No, you'll put pressure on your gears and it'll be extremely painful. But it won't make the slightest bit of difference. You can never undo your past actions, not even when you have a clockwork heart."

I was expecting to be scolded horribly for poking Joe's eye out. But hard as Madeleine tries to look annoyed, she's not entirely successful. And if her voice chokes, it's more with concern than anger. She seems to think it's less serious to poke out a bully's eye than to fall in love.

Strains of "Oh When the Saints" suddenly come our way. It's unusual for Arthur to be paying us a visit at this time of night.

"Och, a carriage full of police officers is making its way up the hill, and they're all looking like their wee minds are set, if ye ken what I mean," he says, out of breath.

"I've got to go, they're coming to find me because of Joe's eye."

A fistful of different emotions sticks in my throat: the rose-tinted dream of finding the little singer combined with my fear of listening to my heart beating against the bars of a prison cell. But a wave of melancholy drowns everything. No more Arthur, no more Anna, no more Luna and, above all, no more Madeleine.

I will come across a few sad looks in the course of my life, but the one Madeleine gives me right now will always be—along with just one other—the saddest I'll ever witness.

"Arthur, go and find Anna and Luna, and try to find a carriage. Jack must leave town as fast as possible. I'll stay here to greet the police."

Arthur plunges into the night, limping as fast as he can to reach the bottom of the mountain.

"I'll get your things ready. You need to be out of here in less than ten minutes."

"What will you tell them?"

"That you haven't come home. And in a few days, I'll say that you've disappeared. You'll be declared dead after a while, and Arthur will help me dig your grave at the foot of your favorite tree, next to Cunnilingus."

"What will you put in the coffin?"

"There won't be a coffin, just an epitaph carved into the tree. The police won't run any checks. That's the advantage of people thinking I'm a witch, they won't go rummaging through my graves."

Madeleine prepares me a bag containing several flasks of tears and a few items of clothing. I don't know how to help her. I could say something meaningful, or fold my underwear, but I'm like a nail stuck in the floorboard.

She hides the second set of keys to my heart by tucking them into my frock coat, so that I can always wind myself up. Then she distributes a few oatcakes wrapped in brown paper among the bag's contents, and hides some books in my trouser pockets.

"I can't carry all that around!"

I'm trying to behave like a grown-up, even if I'm very touched by all this fussing. By way of a response, she flashes me her famous twitch of a smile. No matter what the situation, from the funniest to the most tragic, she always has to make something to eat.

I sit down on my bag, to shut it properly.

"Don't forget, as soon as you've settled down somewhere, you need to make contact with a clockmaker."

"You mean a doctor!"

"Absolutely not! Never go to a doctor if there's something wrong with your heart. No doctor would understand. You'll need to find a clockmaker to sort it out."

I want to tell her how much I love her and how grateful I am, there are so many words jostling on my tongue, but they refuse to cross my lips. All that's left are my arms, so I hug Madeleine tight.

"Careful, you'll hurt your clock if we hug too hard!" she says, in a voice that's gentle and ravaged. "You must go now, I don't want them to find you here."

We pull apart and Madeleine opens the door. I'm still inside the house but I'm already feeling cold.

I get through a whole flask of tears as I run down the familiar path. It lightens my load, but not my heart. I wolf down the oatcakes to soak up the alcohol and my tummy swells up like a pregnant woman's.

On the other side of Arthur's Seat, I can see the police

officers. Joe and his mother are with them. I tremble with a mixture of fear and euphoria.

A carriage is waiting for us at the foot of the mountain. In the glare of the street lamps, it stands out like a piece of the night. Anna, Luna and Arthur clamber in quickly. The coachman, with his mustache stretching all the way to his eyebrows, shouts at his horses in his deep voice. With my cheek pressed against the window, I watch Edinburgh disappearing into the mist.

The lochs extend from hill to hill, measuring out the distance I'm committed to putting behind me. Arthur snores like a steam engine. Anna and Luna dangle their heads; they look like Siamese twins. The tick-tock of my clock echoes in the silence of the night. I realize that this little world of people will set off again without me.

At daybreak, the twisted tune of "Oh When the Saints" wakes me up. I'd never heard it sung so slowly. The carriage has come to a stop.

"We're here!" says Anna.

Luna puts an old birdcage on my knees.

"This is a carrier pigeon that a romantic customer gave me a few years back. It's a very well trained bird. Write to us with your news. Roll your letters around his left claw, and he'll deliver the message to us. We'll be able to stay in touch that way, he'll find you again wherever you are, even in Andalusia, the land where women look you straight in the eye. Good luck, *pequeñito*," she adds, hugging me tightly.

chapter five

In which Little Jack tries to find
a decent clock-doctor in Paris

As the train pulls out of the station, it snorts loudly, making a haunting din. The locomotive's syncopated rhythms set me on edge and my heart might as well be made of popcorn—I'll have to learn to travel better. When I panic, my clockwork heart is like a steam engine turning a bend with its wheels coming unstuck. I'm travelling over the rails of my own fear. What am I frightened of? Of you, Madeleine, or rather, of me without you.

The steam and my own clockwork panic seep under the rails. I want to turn back time, put my old rattletrap of a heart in your arms, Madeleine. Our last hug is still warm, but I'm already as frozen as when I first met you on the coldest day on earth. Oh Madeleine, I hadn't even left the shadows of Edinburgh behind before drinking all your tears. I promise that at the next stop I'll consult a clock-maker. You'll see, I'll come back to you in fine condition, or rather just out of kilter enough for you to exercise your mending talents over me once more.

The more time that goes by, the more this train frightens me, its puffing, rattling heart seems as dilapidated as my own. It must be terrifically in love with its engine. Unless, like me, it's suffering from the sadness of what it's left behind.

I feel alone in my compartment. Madeleine's tears have installed a revolving door inside my head. I'll be sick if I don't speak to somebody. I notice a tall man leaning against the window, writing something. From a distance, he looks like Arthur, but that impression disappears the closer I get. Apart from the shadows he casts, there's nobody near him. Tipsy on loneliness, I launch right in:

"What are you writing, sir?"

The man gives a start and hides his face under his left arm.

"Did I frighten you?"

"You surprised me, it's not the same."

He continues writing, concentrating as hard as if he was painting a picture. The turnstile in my brain starts to pick up speed.

"What do you want, little one?"

"I want to go and win the heart of a woman in Andalusia, but I don't know anything about love. The women I knew never wanted to teach me anything on the subject and I'm feeling all alone in this train . . . I thought perhaps you might be able to help me."

"You've landed on the wrong person, my boy. I'm not very gifted when it comes to love . . . not with living people, at any rate. No, it never really worked out for me with living people."

I start to shudder. I'm reading over his shoulder, which seems to annoy him.

"That red ink . . ."

"It's blood! Go away now, little one, go away!"

He's copying out the same phrase, methodically, on several pieces of paper: *"Your humble servant, Jack the Ripper."*

"We've got the same first name, do you think that's a good sign?"

He shrugs, vexed I'm not more in awe of him. The engine whistles itself hoarse in the distance, the fog creeps through the windows. I'm shivering.

"Go away, little one!"

He strikes the floor with his left heel, the way he might scare a cat. Not that I am one, but it does have a certain effect on me. The sound of his boot competes with that of the train. He turns toward me, his features razor sharp.

"Go away now!"

The fury in his eyes reminds me of Joe. It's like a remote control that switches my legs to tremble mode. He heads toward me.

"Come on, you mists," he drones. "Let the doors of haunted trains slam shut! I'll give you the ghosts of handsome women to carve up in the mist, a twist of blonde or brunette . . ."

His voice becomes a groan.

"I can rip them open without even frightening them . . . signing off your humble servant, Jack the Ripper! Don't be afraid, my boy, you'll soon learn how to survive by frightening others! Don't be afraid, my boy, you'll soon learn how to survive by frightening others . . ."

My heart and body are racing out of control, and this time it's got nothing to do with love. I tear down the train corridors. Nobody. The Ripper chases after me, smashing all the windows with a dagger. A black swarm of birds dives into the compartment, clustering around him. He's making faster progress by walking than I am running.

New compartment. No one around. The racket of his footsteps gets louder. The birds multiply, emerging from his jacket, coming out of his eyes, hurling themselves at me. I jump up onto the seats to put some distance between us; I turn around, and Jack's eyes light up the whole train. The birds are catching up, the shadow of Jack the Ripper looms, and I'm aiming for the driver's door at the end of the carriage. Jack's about to rip out my guts. Oh Madeleine! I can't even hear my own clock ticking anymore, though it's stinging in my chest. The Ripper grabs my shoulder. He's going to kill me, he's going to kill me and I won't have had time to fall in love.

The train slows down. It's pulling into the station.

"Don't be afraid, my boy. You'll soon learn how to survive by frightening others!" Jack the Ripper repeats for a last time, as he stows his weapon away.

I'm trembling with terror. Then he steps off the train and disappears into the crowd of passengers waiting on the platform.

Sitting on a bench at King's Cross station, I begin to come to. The tick-tock of my heart is slowing down, but my clock's wooden casing is still scorching hot. Falling in love can't be as terrifying as finding yourself alone on some ghost train with Jack the Ripper. I thought he was going to kill me. How could a songbird of a girl damage my clock any more than a Ripper? With the tantalizing mischief of her eyes? Her army of extralong eyelashes? The formidable curve of her breasts? Impossible. It can't be as dangerous as what I've just lived through.

A sparrow lands on my minute hand, and I'm startled. Little idiot, he scared me! His feathers gently caress my dial. I'll just wait for him to fly off, then I'll set about leaving Great Britain.

The cross-Channel ferry is less full of nasty surprises than the train to London. Apart from a few elderly ladies who look like faded flowers, nobody seems particularly scary. That said, it takes a while for the mists of melancholy to dissolve. I wind up my heart again with the key, and I feel like I'm turning back time. Or at least turning back my memories. It's the first time in my life I've leaned on memories in this way. I only left the house yesterday, but I feel as if I've been away for ages.

In Paris, I have lunch by the Seine, in a restaurant steaming with the kind of vegetable soups I always love the smell of but hate eating. Plump waitresses smile at me the way people do at babies. Charming old folks chat in hushed voices. I listen to the clatter of saucepan lids and forks. This warm atmosphere reminds me of Dr. Madeleine's old house. I wonder what she's doing on top of the mountain. I decide to write to her:

Dear Madeleine,

Everything is going well, I'm in Paris at the moment. I hope Joe and the police have left you in peace. Don't forget to put the flowers on my grave while you're waiting for me to come back!

I miss you, and the house too.

I'm taking good care of my clock. I'm going to find a clockmaker to help me recover from all these emotions, just as you told me to. Kiss Arthur, Luna and Anna for me.

"Little Jack"

I keep my letter deliberately short, so Luna's pigeon can travel light. I'd like to have some news back as quickly as possible. I roll up my words around the bird's claw and throw him into the Paris sky. He sets off askew. Luna probably tried to give him an original "feather-cut" for when he was courting. She also shaved the sides of his head and, as a result, he looks like a lavatory brush with wings. Perhaps I should have used the conventional postal system.

Before going any further, I need to find a good clockmaker. Since I left home, my heart has been grating louder than ever. I'd like it to be fixed before I find the little singer again. I owe Madeleine that at least. I ring on the door of a jeweller on the Boulevard Saint-Germain. An old man appears, dressed to the nines; he wants to know the reason for my visit.

"To repair my clock . . ."

"Have you brought it with you?"

"Yes!"

I unbutton my jacket, then my shirt.

"I'm not a doctor," he says drily.

"Couldn't you just look at it, to make sure the gears are in the right place?"

"I'm not a doctor, I told you, *I am not a doctor!*"

His tone is haughty, but I try to stay calm. The way he looks at my clock you'd think I was showing him something dirty.

"I know you're not a doctor! This is a perfectly normal clock, which just needs adjusting from time to time to make sure it functions properly . . ."

"Clocks are objects intended to measure time, nothing

else. Get away from here with that diabolical apparatus of yours. Go away, or I'll call the police!"

It's just like at school, or with the young couples, all over again. It may be horribly familiar, but I'll never get used to this feeling of injustice. In fact, the older I get, the more painful it becomes. It's only a bloody wooden clock after all, nothing but gears that allow my heart to beat.

An old metal clock with a thousand pretentious gold-plate flourishes dominates the entrance to the shop. It resembles its owner, in the same way that certain dogs resemble their masters. Just as I'm walking past the door, I give it a good kick, professional footballer style. The clock teeters, its pendulum slamming violently against its sides. As I bolt along the Boulevard Saint-Germain, I hear the tinkle of broken glass behind me. It's amazing how much that sound relaxes me.

The second clockmaker, a fat balding chap in his fifties, seems more sympathetic.

"You should pay a visit to Monsieur Méliès. He's a most inventive illusionist. I'm sure he'll be better placed than I am to sort out your problem, little one."

"I need a clockmaker, not a magician!"

"Some clockmakers have a whiff of the magician about them, but this particular magician has something of the clockmaker about him. He's like the famous Robert-Houdin—whose theater he's just bought," he adds, cheekily. "Pay him a visit and say I sent you. I'm sure he'll fix you up properly!"

I don't understand why this nice gentleman won't mend me himself, but his easy acceptance of my problem is comforting. And I'm keen to meet a magician who's actually a magician-clockmaker. He'll probably look like Madeleine; he might even come from the same family.

I cross the Seine. My eyes nearly pop out at the elegance of the giant cathedral, not to mention the parade of derrières and chignons. This city is a cobblestone wedding cake with a Sacred Heart on top. Finally, I reach the Boulevard des Italiens, where the famous theater is situated. A young man with lively eyes opens the door.

"Does the magician live here?"

"Which one?" he replies, talking in riddles.

"A man called Georges Méliès."

"That's me!"

He walks like an automaton, jerky and elegant at the same time. He speaks quickly, his hands punctuating his words like living exclamation marks. But when I tell him my story, he listens very carefully. Above all, it's the conclusion that interests him:

"Even if this clock functions as my heart, the maintenance work I'm asking of you is straightforward for a clockmaker."

As the clockmaker-conjurer opens my dial, he listens to my chest with a stethoscope that allows him to hear the

minuscule elements. His attitude softens, as if his childhood is flashing before his eyes. He activates the system,
setting off the clockwork cuckoo, then promptly expresses
his admiration for Madeleine's work.

"How did you manage to bend the hour hand?" he asks.

"I'm in love but I don't know anything about love. So I
get angry, I get into fights, and sometimes I even try to
speed time up or else to slow it down. Is it badly damaged?"

He laughs like a child, except he's got a mustache.

"No, everything's working very nicely. What exactly did
you want to know?"

"Well, Dr. Madeleine, who fitted me with this clock, says
that my makeshift heart isn't suitable for falling in love.
She's convinced it wouldn't survive such an emotional
shock."

"Really? I see . . ."

He screws up his eyes and strokes his chin.

"That might be her opinion . . . but you don't have to
share it, do you?"

"I don't agree with her, you're right. But when I saw the
little singer for the first time, I felt as if an earthquake was
going on underneath my clock. The gears grated, my tick-
tock sped up. I started suffocating, getting myself all tan-
gled up, everything was topsy-turvy."

"Did you like that?"

"I loved it."

"Ah! So what was the problem?"

"Well, I was terrified Madeleine might be right."

Georges Méliès shakes his head and strokes his mustache. He's searching for the right words, the way a surgeon might choose his instruments.

"If you're frightened of damaging yourself, you increase the risk of doing just that. Consider the tightrope walker. Do you think he spares any thought for falling while he's walking the rope? No, he accepts the risk, and enjoys the thrill of braving the danger. If you spend your whole life being careful not to break anything, you'll get terribly bored, you know . . . I can't think of anything more fun than being impulsive. Just look at you! I only have to say the word 'impulsive' and your eyes light up. Aha! When a person aged fourteen decides to cross Europe to track down a girl, that means that they've got rather a taste for impulsiveness, doesn't it?"

"Yes, yes . . . But have you got something that would make my heart a bit more robust?"

"Of course I have. Listen to me carefully. Are you ready? Listen to me very carefully: the only thing, as you say, that will allow you to seduce the woman of your dreams is your heart. Not the clockwork version that was grafted on to you at birth. I'm talking about the real one, the one that's underneath, made of flesh and blood, pulsing. That's the one you've got to work with. Forget about your clockwork problems and they'll seem less important. Be impulsive and above all give, give without counting the cost."

Méliès is very expressive. All his features are active when he speaks. Catlike, his mustache follows his smile.

"It doesn't work every time. I'm not guaranteeing anything. Take me, for example: I've just failed with the woman I thought was the love of my life. There simply is no trick that works every time."

I've been given a lesson in love by a conjurer (some might call him a genius) who's just confessed that his most recent potion blew up in his face. But I have to concede that his words are doing me as much good as his adjustments to my gears. He's gentle and he knows how to listen. You can tell he understands the way that humans work. Perhaps he's succeeded in penetrating the secrets of man's psychological machinery. In just a few hours, we've struck up a friendly alliance.

"I could write a book about your story. I know it as well as if it was my own now," he tells me.

"So write it. If I have children one day, they'll be able to read it. But if you want to find out what happens next, you'll have to come with me to Andalusia."

"Surely you don't want a depressed conjurer accompanying you on your pilgrimage of love?"

"Actually yes, I'd like that a lot."

"You know I might mess up a miracle?"

"Of course you won't."

"Give me the night to mull it over, will you?"

"It's a deal."

As the first rays of sunshine begin to sneak through the shutters of Georges Méliès's workshop, I hear shouting:

"¡Andalusia! ¡Anda! ¡Andalusia! ¡Anda! ¡AndaaaAAAH!"

A madman in pajamas appears, straight out of an opera.

"All right, young man. I could do with 'travelling' in every sense of the word, I'm not going to let myself be crushed by my misery forever. A great blast of fresh air, that's what we're both going to enjoy! If you still want me as a companion, that is."

"Of course! When are we leaving?"

"Straightaway, after breakfast!" he answers, pointing to his travel bag.

We sit down at a rickety table to drink scalding hot chocolate and eat jam on toast that's too soft. It's not as tasty as one of Madeleine's breakfasts, but it's fun to be eating in the midst of paper cutout extraterrestrials.

"You know, when I was in love, I was always inventing things. A whole array of tricks, illusions and optical effects to amuse my lady friend. I think she'd had enough of my inventions by the end," he says, his mustache at half-mast. "I wanted to create a voyage to the moon just for her, but what I should have given her was a real journey on earth. I should have asked for her hand in marriage, found us a house that was easier to live in than my old workshop, and I don't know what else . . ." he sighs. "One day, I sawed two planks from the shelves and attached wheels rescued from a hospital trolley, so that the two of us could glide in the moonlight. I called them 'roller-boards.' But she never wanted to climb onto them. And I had to repair the shelves too. Love isn't easy every day, my boy," he repeats, dreamily. "But you and I, we'll climb onto those boards! We'll speed across half of Europe on our roller-boards!"

"Can we catch trains as well? Because I'm a bit pressed for time . . ."

"Oppressed by time?"

"That too."

To think that my clock is a magnet for broken hearts: Madeleine, Arthur, Anna, Luna, even Joe; and now Méliès. I get the impression their hearts need the care of a good clockmaker even more than mine does.

chapter six

Wind-battered mustaches,
empty claws, and a fiery flamenco sauce

Southward! Here we are, setting off along the roads of France, pilgrims on wheels chasing an impossible dream. What a pair we make: one of us tall and gangly with a mustache like a cat's whiskers, the other a short redhead with a wooden heart. Don Quixote and Sancho Panza, we lay siege to the spaghetti western landscape of Andalusia. Luna used to describe the south of Spain as an unpredictable place where dreams and nightmares coexist, like cowboys and Indians in the American Wild West. *¡Qué será será!*

.   .   .

Along the way, we talk a great deal. In some ways Méliès has become my Dr. Love, playing the opposite role to Madeleine; and yet, they remind me of each other. I try to encourage him to win back his sweetheart.

"She might still be in love with you, wherever she is. And she'd still enjoy a voyage to the moon, wouldn't she, even if it was in a cardboard rocket?"

"I'm afraid not. She says I'm pathetic, the way I'm always tinkering with things. She's bound to fall in love with a scientist or a soldier, given how it all ended."

My conjurer-clockmaker has a wry outlook even when he's drowning in sorrow. His wonky, wind-battered mustache could tell you that.

I've never laughed as much as I do in the course of this fabulous ride. We travel like stowaways on freight trains, sleep very little and eat whatever we can get our hands on. I may have a clock for a heart, but I've given up keeping an eye on the time. We are rained on so often that I can't believe we haven't shrunk. But nothing can stop us. We feel more alive than ever.

When we reach Lyon, we cross the Pont de la Guillotière on our roller-boards, holding on to the back of a carriage, and passers-by cheer us as if we were the peloton in the Tour de France.

In Valence, after a night spent roaming the streets, an old lady treats us like her grandsons and cooks up the most delicious *poulet-frites* in the world. We're also allowed a soapy bath that works wonders, and a glass of still lemonade. The high life.

Feeling clean and perky, we set off to attack the Gates of the South. The city of Orange and its railway police who don't want to let us sleep in the livestock vans; Perpignan with its early smells of Spain. Kilometer by kilometer, my dream grows thick with possibilities. Miss Acacia, I'm coming!

I feel invincible travelling alongside Captain Méliès. Buttressed against our roller-boards, we cross the Spanish border, and a warm wind rushes inside me, transforming my clock hands into windmill blades. They'll grind the seeds of my dreams and turn them into reality. Miss Acacia, I'm coming!

An army of olive trees ushers us through, followed by orange trees nestling their fruit in the sky. Tireless, we press on. The red mountains of Andalusia slice through our horizon.

A cumulus cloud ruptures on those mountain peaks, spitting its nervous lightning a few hundred meters away from us. Méliès signals that I should tuck my scrap metal away. Now is not the moment to conduct lightning.

A bird approaches, hovering like a vulture. The circle of rocks surrounding us gives him a sinister air. But it's just Luna's old carrier pigeon, bringing me news from Edinburgh. I'm so relieved to see him back at last. Despite my simmering dreams of Miss Acacia, I haven't forgotten about Dr. Madeleine for a moment.

The pigeon lands in a tiny cloud of dust. My heart races, I'm impatient to read the letter. But I can't catch the wretched bird. My mustachioed Indian friend tries to tame him by cooing away, and eventually I grab hold of his feathery body.

But it's all a waste of time. The pigeon is travelling empty-clawed, with just a remnant of string on his left leg. And no letter from Madeleine; the wind must have snatched it. Perhaps in the Rhône Valley around Valence, where the gusts rush in before sloping off to die in the sun.

I feel as disappointed as if I'd just opened a parcel full of ghosts. I perch on my roller-board and hastily scribble a note.

Dear Madeleine,

In your next letter, please could you let me know what you said in your first, because this idiot pigeon went and lost it before delivering it to me.

I've found a clockmaker who is taking good care of my clock, and I'm doing well.

I miss you lots. Anna, Luna and Arthur too.

With love from
Jack

Méliès helps me roll the piece of paper correctly around the bird's claw.

"If she knew I was at the gates of Andalusia, chasing after my love, she'd be furious."

"All mothers are afraid for their children and protect them as best they can, but it's time for you to leave the nest. Look at your heart! It's midday! We've got to push on. Have you seen what's written on the sign straight ahead? *'¡Granada!' ¡Anda! ¡Anda!'* Méliès roars, with an otherworldly glimmer in his eye.

In a treasure hunt, when the glow from the gold coins starts to glimmer through the keyhole in the chest, the seeker is overcome by emotion, barely able to open the lid. Fear of winning.

As for me, I've been nursing this dream for so long. Joe smashed it against my head, and I picked up the pieces. Patiently, I endured the pain, but in my imagination I was already putting the egg back together again, and it was full of pictures of the little singer. Now here she is, about to hatch, and I'm rigid with stage fright. The Alhambra extends its arabesques toward us, outlined against the opal sky. The carriages jolt about. My clock jolts too. The wind picks up, blowing dust all around and lifting up the women's dresses, turning them into parasols. Will I dare to open you out, Miss Acacia?

As soon as we arrive in the old city, we set about hunting down its theaters. The light is almost blinding. Méliès asks the same question at every theater we find along the way:

"Does a little flamenco-singing girl with poor eyesight ring any bells?"

It'd be easier to spot a snowflake in a snowstorm. Dusk

finally calms the city's orangey-red glow, but still there's no trace of Miss Acacia.

"There are lots of singing girls like that around here . . ." replies a skinny man sweeping the square in front of the umpteenth theater.

"No, no, no, this one is *extraordinary.* She's very young, fourteen or fifteen years old, but she sings like a grown woman. Oh, and she's always bumping into things."

"If she really is as extraordinary as you say she is, then you should try the Extraordinarium."

"What's that?"

"An old circus converted into a funfair. They've got every kind of show there: caravans of troubadours, prima ballerinas, ghost trains, carousels of wild elephants, sing-ing birds, freak shows of real-life monsters . . . I think they might have a little singing girl. It's at 7, calle Pablo Jardim, in the Cartuja district, about a quarter of an hour from here."

"Thank you very much, sir."

"It's a curious place, but if you like that kind of thing . . . Good luck, anyway!"

On the road leading to the Extraordinarium, Méliès is full of last-minute recommendations.

"Play it like a poker game. Never reveal your fears or doubts. You've got a trump card and it's called your heart. You may think of it as a weakness, but embrace your vul-nerability and your clockwork heart will make you special. It's precisely your difference that will win her over."

"My handicap will be a weapon of seduction? Do you really think so?"

"Of course! Don't tell me that you weren't charmed by that singer of yours when she refused to put on her glasses? When she began bumping into things?"

"Oh, it's not that . . ."

"It's not *just* that, of course, but her 'difference' is all part of her charm. And now is the time to make the most of yours."

It's ten o'clock at night by the time we enter the Extraordinarium. We travel up and down the alleyways as music rings out from every corner, several melodies blending together in a joyful brouhaha. Stalls give off a smell of frying and dust—people must be thirsty all the time here.

The crackpot collection of fairground attractions looks set to topple at the slightest puff. The House of Singing Birds is just like my heart, only bigger. You have to wait for the hour to strike in order to see those birds popping out from behind the dial; it's easier to adjust a clock when there's nothing alive inside.

After wandering around for some time, I notice a wall with a poster announcing that evening's shows, complete with photos.

Miss ACACIA

FIERY FLAMENCO SAUCE

10 P.M.

ON THE SMALL STAGE

OPPOSITE THE GHOST TRAIN

I recognize her features instantly. I've been searching in my dreams for four years, and now, right at the end of the race, reality is finally taking over. I feel dizzy, like a fledgling bird on the day it first takes flight. The cozy nest of my imagination is receding; it's time to jump.

The paper roses stitched on to the little singer's dress trace the treasure map that is her body. The tip of my tongue tastes electric. I'm a bomb ready to explode—a terrified bomb, but a bomb all the same.

We head toward the stage, and take our seats. The stage is a simple platform set up under a trailer awning. To think that in a few moments I'm about to see her . . . How many millions of seconds have been and gone since my tenth birthday? How many millions of times have I dreamt of this moment? The euphoria is so intense I'm finding it hard to stay still. Meanwhile, inside my chest, the proud windmill has reverted to a tiny Swiss cuckoo.

The spectators in the front row turn toward me, annoyed by the increasingly audible racket my clock is making. Méliès responds with his catlike smile. Three girls burst out laughing and say something in Spanish, presumably along the lines of: "those two just escaped from the freak show." It's true our clothes could do with a good ironing.

The little singer walks onstage, clicking her yellow high heels along the platform. She launches into her bird dance and my clock hands become windmill blades once again: I'm flying! Her voice echoes like a slender nightingale, sounding even more beautiful than in my dreams. I want to take the time to watch her calmly, to adjust my heart to her presence.

Miss Acacia arches the small of her back and her lips part a little, as if being kissed by a ghost. She closes her large eyes as she claps her raised hands like castanets.

During a particularly intimate song, my cuckoo whirrs into action. I'm more embarrassed than ever. The twinkle in Méliès's eyes helps to calm me down.

We're in such a rundown place, yet the little singer transcends our surroundings. You'd think she was lighting her own Olympic flame in a plastic model stadium.

At the end of the show, she's mobbed by all sorts of people wanting to exchange a word or get her autograph. I have to queue like everybody else, even though I'm not asking for an autograph, just the moon. The two of us curled up in its crescent. Méliès tips me off:

"Her dressing-room door is open and there's nobody inside!"

I slip in like a burglar.

Closing the door of the tiny dressing room behind me, I take a moment to study her makeup, her sequined ankle boots and her wardrobe—Tinker Bell would have approved. I'm embarrassed to be looking at her personal belongings, but it's delicious to be this close to her. As I perch on her chaise longue, her delicate perfume intoxicates me. I wait.

The door bursts open and the little singer enters like a hurricane in a skirt. Her yellow shoes go flying. Hairpins rain down. She sits in front of her dressing table. I am more silent than the deadest of corpses.

She starts taking off her makeup, as delicately as a pink snake might shed its skin, and then puts on a pair of glasses. She sees my reflection in the mirror.

"What are you doing in here?" she demands.

Please forgive this intrusion. Ever since I heard you singing some years ago, my only dream has been to find you again. I've crossed half of Europe to get here. I've had eggs smashed on my head. And I've nearly had my guts ripped out by a man who only fell in love with dead women. There's no doubt about it, I'm handicapped by my great love. My makeshift heart isn't strong enough to resist the emotional earthquake I feel when I see you, but here it is, bursting for you. That's what I'm desperate to say. Instead I'm silent as an orchestra of tombstones.

"How did you manage to get in?"

She's furious, but shock seems to dilute her anger. She discreetly removes her glasses and I can tell she's curious now.

"Be careful," Méliès had warned me. "She's a singer, she's pretty, you won't be the first to feel this way about her . . . The masterstroke of your seduction must be to create the illusion that you're not trying to seduce her."

I'm flustered. I don't know what to say. "I leaned against your door and it wasn't closed properly, so I landed on your dressing-room sofa," I finally tell her, realizing how ridiculous it sounds.

"Do you make a habit of landing in the dressing rooms of girls who need to get changed?"

"No, no, not often."

Each word I say is monumentally important, emerging with difficulty, syllable by syllable; I can feel the full weight of the dream I'm carrying.

"Where do you normally show up? In the bed or the bath?"

"I don't normally show up anywhere."

I try to remember the lesson in rose-tinted magic that Méliès taught me, for romance: *Show her who you really are, make her laugh or cry, but pretend you want to be her friend. Be interested in her, not just her derrière. We don't hold a candle to someone for as long when we're only after their derrière, do we?*

Which is true, but now that I've seen how her derrière moves, I rather fancy it, which complicates matters.

"Weren't you the one who made that devil of a racket with your tick-tock during the concert? In fact, don't I recognize you . . ."

"Recognize me?"

"Look, what do you want from me?"

I take a deep breath, using up all the air that's left in my lungs.

"I wanted to give you something. It's not flowers, and it's not chocolate either . . ."

"So what is it?"

I produce the bunch of spectacles from my bag, trying not to tremble as I hold the frames out to her. But I can't help it, the makeshift bouquet clinks and rattles.

Miss Acacia makes a face like a sulky doll. Her expression could be disguising laughter or anger, and I don't know what to make of it. The bunch of glasses weighs a ton. I'm going to get cramp, plus I look ridiculous.

"What is it?"

"A bouquet of glasses."

"They're not my favorite flowers." On the edge of the world, somewhere between her chin and the parting of her lips, a microscopic smile glimmers.

"Thank you, but I'd like to get dressed in peace now."

She opens the door for me, the light from the street lamp dazzles her. I position my hands between the street lamp and her eyes. I see her forehead unfurrow. It's a moment of delicious turmoil.

"I don't like wearing glasses. I've got a small head and they make me look like a fly."

"That's fine by me."

Mentioning the fly is her ploy to defuse that delicious turmoil; but my answer reactivates it. The brief silence that follows is as tender as a rainstorm of daisies.

"Could we see each other again, with or without the spectacles?"

chapter seven

In which Little Jack spends his first night in the Extraordinarium, and encounters an ostrich in an extremely bad mood

Miss Acacia's tiny "yes" could have emerged from a fledgling's beak, but for me, it's a surge of heroic energy. The romantic thrills have begun; my tick-tock sounds like the beads of a necklace clinking between her fingers. Nothing can dent my mood.

"She accepted your bouquet of twisted glasses?" asks Méliès. "So she likes you! She *must* like you! No one would accept such a pathetic present if they didn't have feelings for you," he beams.

After regaling Méliès with every detail of our first impromptu encounter, and once my euphoria has subsided, I ask him to check on my clock, because I've never felt such intense emotions. Madeleine, how furious you'd be . . . Méliès smiles his big mustachioed grin and then gently starts to manipulate my gears.

"Does it hurt anywhere?"

"No, I don't think so."

"Your gears are rather hot, but not unusually so. Otherwise everything's in perfect working order. Come on, let's go. Affairs of the heart are all very well, but we need a good bath and somewhere to sleep!"

After exploring the Extraordinarium, we settle into an abandoned stall for the night. Despite our dilapidated surroundings and our growling stomachs, we sleep like babies.

At dawn, my mind is made up: I've got to find a job so that I can stay here.

But all the jobs have been taken at the Extraordinarium. All the jobs except one that is, in the Ghost Train, where they need someone to scare the passengers. Sheer persistence gets me an interview with the manager for the following evening.

Seeing as he's got nothing better to do, Méliès performs a few old tricks at the entrance with his set of hoax cards. He's a hit, especially with the ladies. His *belles,* as he likes to call them, form a huddle around his table and marvel at his every sleight of hand. He tells them that he plans to create a story in motion, a sort of photographic book that will spring to life. He knows how to capture the imagination of his *belles*.

This morning, I saw him collecting cardboard boxes and cutting rockets out of them. I think he still hopes to win back his fiancée. He's even started talking about the voyage to the moon again. His dream machine is gently revving into action.

It's six o'clock when I arrive at the great stone entrance to the Ghost Train. I'm greeted by the manager, a shrivelled old lady who answers to the name of Brigitte Heim.

Her face is so tight that you'd think she was gripping a knife between her teeth. She's wearing big sad shoes— nun's sandals—that are ideal for trampling on dreams.

"So, you want to work on the Ghost Train, do you, dwarf?"

Her voice reminds me of an ostrich, an ostrich in an extremely bad mood. She has the knack of inducing a sickening sense of panic the moment you meet her.

Jack the Ripper's last words echo in my head: "You'll soon learn how to survive by frightening others!"

I unbutton my shirt and turn the key in my lock to make the cuckoo sing. Brigitte Heim watches me with the same disdain as the clockmaker in Paris.

"You're not going to earn us a fortune with that! But I haven't got anybody else, so I'll take you."

Desperate for the work, I swallow my pride.

My new boss embarks on a tour of her premises.

"I have an agreement with the cemetery: I collect the skulls and bones of the dead whose families can no longer pay for their burial plot," she says, proudly showing me around. "They make rather good decorations for a ghost train, don't you think? And anyway, if I didn't collect them, they'd be tossed on to the rubbish heap!" she declares, in a voice that's creaky and hysterical.

Skulls and spiders' webs have been methodically arranged to filter the light from the candelabras. There's not a speck of dust anywhere else, and nothing out of place. I wonder what extraterrestrial emptiness makes this woman spend her life cleaning catacombs.

"Do you have children?" I ask, turning toward her.

"What kind of a question is that? No, I have a dog, and I'm very happy with my dog."

If I end up growing old one day and I'm lucky enough to have children, and why not grandchildren too, I'd like to build houses full of little people chasing each other, laughing and shouting. But if I don't have offspring, then houses full of nothing won't be for me.

"Touching the décor is strictly forbidden," she tells me, showing me around. "If you walk on a skull and break it, you have to pay!"

Pay, her favorite word.

She wants to know my reason for coming to Granada. I rattle off my story. Or rather I try to, but she keeps cutting me off.

"I don't believe in this clockwork heart business, or in

your love story full stop. I wonder who made you fall for such nonsense? I suppose you think you'll work wonders with this trinket? Well, mark my words, you may be short but you'll fall from a great height! People don't stray far; they don't like anything that's different. And even if they enjoy the show, it's because of a voyeuristic pleasure. To them, going to see the woman with two heads is the same as witnessing an accident. I've known many men applaud, but not one fall in love. It'll be the same for you. People might be fascinated by your wounded heart, but that won't make them love you for who you are. Do you really think a pretty young girl like the one you've just described to me would want to get involved with a boy who's got a prosthesis instead of a heart? Personally, I'd have found it a complete turnoff . . . But enough of that: as long as you can frighten my customers, everyone's happy."

The ghastly Brigitte Heim rejoins her coven of doom-sayers. But she has no idea what a thick shell of dreams I've been building ever since I was small. As I head off into the night to gobble the moon, which looks like a phosphorescent pancake, I'm dreaming of Miss Acacia. Heim can stalk me with her living-dead rictus all she likes, but she'll never steal anything from me.

Ten o'clock. I turn up for my first evening's work. The train is half full and I've got to be onstage in half an hour. It's time to try my hand as a Scareperson. The thing

is, I'm a bit terrified myself, because I need to hold on
to this job if I want to remain the little singer's official
neighbor.

I get my heart ready, transforming it into a terrifying
instrument. Up on top of the mountain at Dr. Madeleine's,
I used to have fun stuffing all sorts of things inside my
clock: pebbles, newspaper, marbles . . . The gears would
start screeching, the tick-tock became chaotic, and the
cuckoo impersonated a miniature bulldozer lumbering
around my lungs. It used to horrify Madeleine.

Half-past ten. I'm glued to the wall of the last carriage,
like an Indian ready to attack a stagecoach. Brigitte Heim
watches me out of the corner of her menacing eye. Imagine my surprise when I notice Miss Acacia calmly sitting
in one of the Ghost Train carriages. My stage fright intensifies, making my tick-tock sputter.

The train sets off, I leap from carriage to carriage, and
there she is—my conquest of the Amorous West. I've got
to put in a consummate performance. My life is at stake. I
hurl myself against the carriage walls, my cuckoo clock rattling inside me like a popcorn machine. I glide my icy
hour hand against the customers' backs, and think of
Arthur as I start to sing "Oh When the Saints." A few people shout: "What can you do to scare us?" I just want to
escape my own body and project sunlight on to the walls
for *her* to see, so she warms up and yearns for my arms.
But instead, as a kind of finale, I appear in the white light
for a few seconds, thrusting out my chest in exaggerated

fashion. I open my shirt, so people can see the gears moving beneath my skin with each heartbeat. My performance is greeted by an astonishing goat's shriek from a lady of mature years, and three rounds of fake applause littered with laughter.

I watch Miss Acacia, hoping that somehow I might have pleased her.

She smiles like a mischievous sweet-snatcher.

"Is it over? . . . Ah, very good, I didn't see a thing, but everybody seemed to think it was highly entertaining, congratulations! I didn't know it was you, but bravo!"

"Thank you . . . and what about the glasses, have you tried them on?"

"Yes. But they're all bent or broken . . ."

"I chose them like that, so you could wear them without worrying about breaking them!"

"You think I don't wear glasses because I'm worried about breaking them?"

"No . . ."

She has this gentle way of laughing, as light as beads tumbling over a xylophone.

"Last stop, everybody off!" screeches the ostrich in charge.

The little singer gets up and waves at me discreetly. Her curly hair ripples over her curvy shadow. I wish I could have scared her just a teeny bit, but I'm relieved she didn't get to see what my heart looks like. It doesn't matter that I'm a shining sun when I dream at night, old Brigitte has woken my old demons. The toughest carapace in the world sometimes softens in the grip of insomnia.

In the distance, Miss Acacia's high heels tinkle rhythmically. I relish their sound until I hear my little singer crashing into the exit door. Everybody laughs and nobody helps her. She totters like a well-dressed soak, then disappears.

Meanwhile, Brigitte Heim has launched into a critique of my performance that goes right over my head, but I think at one point she does utter the words *"pay you."*

I can't wait to catch up with Méliès and tell him all about it. Thrusting my hand into my pockets as I head off, I discover a scrap of paper rolled up into a ball.

I don't need glasses to see how accomplished your performance is. Your appointments diary must run to several volumes . . . Will you be able to find the page where you wrote my name?

I make the conjurer who tends to my heart read the message, between two rounds of cards.

"Hmm, I see . . . your Miss Acacia isn't like the other singers I've known, she's not self-centered. That means she's not entirely aware of her seductive powers—which is no doubt part of her charm. Then again, she spotted your act. It's all or nothing now, you don't have anything to lose. And remember, she doesn't realize how desirable she is. Use that to your advantage!"

.   .   .

I head over to her dressing room and slide a note under her door:

> *On the stroke of midnight behind the Ghost Train, wait for me, and wear your glasses so you don't bump into the moon. I promise I'll give you enough time to take them off before I look at you.*

"*¡Anda, hombre! ¡Anda!* It's time to show her your heart!" says Méliès again.

"I'm worried about frightening her with my clock hands. I don't know what I'll do if she rejects me. Do you realize how long I've been dreaming of this moment?"

"Remember what I told you, show her your real heart. That's the only magic you can perform. If she sees your real heart, your clock won't frighten her, believe me!"

While I'm waiting for midnight like a lover impatient for Christmas, Luna's battered pigeon lands on my shoulder. This time, the letter hasn't got lost. I unfold it in great excitement.

> *My Little Jack,*
>
> *We trust you're coping well and taking good care of yourself. You'll have to wait a while longer before coming back to the house because of the police.*

Lovingly,
Dr. Madeleine

I'm overjoyed at the arrival of the pigeon, but the contents of the letter he's carried all this way are ever so frustrating. There's something odd about that signature: Dr. Madeleine. And I'd have expected her to be more chatty. She probably wanted to spare her messenger. Still, I feel a twinge of guilt. If Madeleine knew what I was up to tonight, how furious she'd be . . . I send the bird straight back:

Send me some long letters by normal post, I may stay
here for some time. I miss you. I want to read more than
a few words attached to a pigeon's leg. Everything's
going well over here, I've got a job and am friends with a
clockmaker-conjurer who makes sure my heart is
working properly. You can send your letters to his
workshop—he always knows where to find me. Are the
police leaving you alone? Write back quickly!

With love,
Jack

PS—c/o Monsieur Méliès, The Extraordinarium, 7, calle
Pablo Jardim, La Cartuja, Granada

Midnight, I'm waiting like a happy idiot. I'm wearing an electric-blue jumper, a sort of vitamin kick for my green eyes. The Ghost Train is silent.

Twenty past midnight, nothing. Half-past midnight, still no sign of Miss Acacia. At twenty to one, my heart is growing cold, and the tick-tock is dwindling.

"Hey!"

"I'm over here . . ."

She stands poised on the walkway, perfectly balanced on the doormat. Even her shadow against the door is sexy; I'd happily get in some kissing practice with *that,* for starters . . .

"I've come disguised as you, without even realizing it!" says the real Miss Acacia.

She's wearing a thick sweater almost identical to mine.

"I'm sorry, I didn't have time to find a proper outfit for our date, but it looks like you had the same problem!"

I smile, even though I've pulled out all the sartorial stops. I can't help staring at the way her lips move. I sense she picks up on this. As she listens to the noises produced by my clock, the silences between our words grow longer. It's as if an angel is passing overhead, but then she goes and decapitates it:

"You're a hit on the Ghost Train, all the girls came out smiling."

"That's not a good sign, I'm supposed *to survive by frightening others* . . . I mean, that's what I've got to do if I want to keep my job here."

"Does it really matter whether you make them laugh or cry, as long as you're getting a reaction?"

"That old bag Brigitte told me it wouldn't do the Ghost

Train's image any good if people came out giggling. I think I'll have to learn how to scare people if I want to keep on working there."

"Scaring is just another form of seduction . . . and as far as seducing people is concerned, it looks like you're doing a pretty good job."

I want to tell her I've got a prosthesis instead of a heart and I don't know anything about love. I want her to understand that I'm feeling these emotions for the first time. Yes, I know I've had a few lessons in romantic magic with an illusionist, but that was just to help me find her. I want to seduce her without her mistaking me for a skirt-chaser. It's a delicate balancing act. So all I say is:

"I'd like to hold you in my arms."

Silence, a new sulky doll pout, eyes shut.

"We could keep talking about it afterward, but can we hold each other first?"

Miss Acacia lets out an "all right" so tiny it barely escapes her lips. A tender silence falls over our gestures. She teeters toward me. Close up, she's even more beautiful than her shadow—and more intimidating too. I pray to some unknown deity to keep my clock from chiming.

Our arms interlace and become one. I'm embarrassed by my clock, and I don't dare crush my chest against hers. I don't want to scare her with my bric-a-brac heart. But how can I avoid frightening this little bird of a woman when my sharp clock hands jut out from my lungs? My clockwork panic whirrs into action again.

. . .

I'm avoiding her with my left side, as if I had a glass heart. This makes our dance more complicated, especially as she appears to be a tango champion. The volume of my tick-tock rises from inside me; Madeleine's warnings flash through my mind. What if I die before I've even kissed Miss Acacia? I feel like I'm jumping into the unknown: joy of flying, fear of going splat.

Her fingers are languid behind my neck and my own are pleasantly lost somewhere beneath her shoulder blades. I try to solder my dreams to reality, but I'm working without a protective mask. Our mouths draw closer. Time slows, until it has almost ground to a halt. Our lips take over, in the softest relay race in the world; they mingle, delicately and intensely. It feels as though her tongue is a sparrow gently landing on mine; curiously, she tastes of strawberries.

I watch as she hides her huge eyes under the parasols of her eyelids. I feel like a weight lifter, with the Himalayas on my left arm and the Rockies on my right; Atlas is a hard-working dwarf by comparison. A giant wave of joy engulfs me. The train's ghosts echo with each of our gestures. We're wrapped inside the sound made by her heels tapping against the floor.

"Silence!" shrieks a vinegary voice.

Brusquely, we pull apart. It seems we've woken the Loch Ness Monster. We don't dare breathe.

"Is that you, midget? What are you up to on the premises at this hour?"

"I'm trying to find new ways of scaring people."

"Well, find them in silence. And don't touch my brand-new skulls!"

"Yes, yes . . ."

Terrified, Miss Acacia buries herself deeper in my arms. Time has come to a standstill and I've got no desire for it to pick up its normal pace again. I even forget about keeping my heart at a distance. Laying her head against my chest, she suddenly makes a face.

"What's under there? It's hurting me!"

I don't answer, I just break out in a cold sweat. She's found me out. I consider lying, making something up, faking it, but there's so much sincerity in her question that I can't bring myself to do that. I open my shirt slowly, button by button. The clock appears, and the tick-tock resounds more loudly. I await my sentencing. She brings her hand near, murmuring:

"What is it?"

The compassion in her voice is enough to make me want to be an invalid for the rest of my days, just to have her as a nurse by my side. The cuckoo begins to sing. She jumps. Turning the key, I whisper:

"I'm sorry. It's my secret. I wanted to tell you about it sooner, but I was scared of frightening you for good."

I explain to her that this clock has functioned as my heart since the day I was born. I don't say anything about love—along with anger—being strictly off limits. She asks if my feelings would alter if the clock were changed, or whether this would simply be a mechanical operation.

There's something malicious in her voice; she seems to find it all rather amusing. I explain that my clockwork heart can't function without emotions, but I don't venture any further into that slippery terrain.

She smiles, as if I'm explaining the rules of a fabulous game. No cries of horror, no laughter. Until now, Arthur, Anna, Luna and Méliès are the only people who haven't been shocked by my clockwork heart. I take it as an important love token, the way she seems to be saying: *So you've got a cuckoo between your bones? AND?* Simple, so simple . . .

But I mustn't get too carried away. Perhaps it's just that the clock looks less repulsive through her defective eyes.

"That's very handy. If you grow weary of love as all men do, I could try replacing your heart before you replace me with another woman."

"According to the clock in my heart, we kissed for the first time exactly thirty-seven minutes ago, so I think we've still got a bit of time ahead of us before we need to think about that sort of thing."

Even when she's telling me that she's no pushover, there's something gracious about the way she does it.

I accompany Miss Acacia on tiptoe back home, stealthy as a wolf. I embrace her like a wolf, and like a wolf I disappear into the night.

I've just kissed the girl with the voice of a nightingale and nothing will ever be the same again. My clock is pulsing like an impetuous volcano. But nothing hurts. Apart from a stitch in my side which is a small price to pay, though, for being drunk on such joy. Tonight, I'm going to climb to the moon and make myself comfortable in its crescent, as if I were slung in a hammock. And when I dream it won't be because I'm asleep.

chapter eight

In which our hero solders his dreams to reality and finds the entry code to Miss Acacia's heart

The next day, Brigitte Heim wakes me with her witch's voice devoid of charm.

"Get up, midget! Today you'd better start frightening people, or I'm kicking you out on no pay."

First thing in the morning, her vinegary voice makes me feel sick. I've got a lover's hangover; and waking up is a shock to the system.

Perhaps I got dreams and reality muddled up last night? Next time, will I still be able to feel that fizz of excitement? Just thinking about it makes my clock tingle. I know I'm blatantly disregarding Madeleine's advice. I've never felt so happy, or so distraught.

I go to see Méliès to get my clock checked.

"Your heart has never worked better, my boy," he reassures me. "If you could only see yourself in the mirror as you talked about what happened last night, you'd know from your eyes that your heart's barometer is showing fair weather."

All day long I drift about the Ghost Train, thinking about how I'll play alchemist again this evening, transforming my dream into reality.

We only see each other at night. Miss Acacia's proud coquettishness gives her away, because she always bumps into something. It's her way of knocking on the door of the Ghost Train.

We love each other like two matches in the dark. We don't talk, we just catch fire instead. Our kisses are an inferno as an earthquake registers across my entire body, all one meter sixty-six and a half centimeters of it. My heart escapes its prison. It flies away through the arteries, settling in my head. My heart is in every muscle, all the way through to my fingertips. A savage sun, everywhere. It's a romantic disease with reddish glints.

I can't survive without her; the scent of her skin, the sound of her voice, the mannerisms that make her the strongest and most fragile girl in the world. Take her obsession with not wearing glasses, so she only gets to look at the world through the smokescreen of her damaged sight; perhaps it's a form of self-protection? That way she can see without really seeing and, more importantly, without knowing when she's being watched.

I learn about the strange mechanics of her heart: a protective outer shell hides her mysterious lack of confidence, whereby low self-esteem is constantly vying with the sheer force of her determination. The sparks that fly when Miss Acacia sings are fiery splinters of the soul. She can project this confidence onstage, but as soon as the music stops the balance tilts the other way. I haven't yet found the broken gear inside her.

The entry code to her heart changes every evening. Sometimes, the shell is as hard as a rock. I might try a thousand combinations in the form of caresses and comforting words, but I'm stuck at the door. What a treat when I do eventually crack the combination. To hear her tiny sigh of surrender, I gently blow and her outer shell flies off in a thousand pieces.

"How to tame a shooting star. That's the instruction manual I need," I tell Méliès.

"A handbook of pure alchemy, you mean . . . Ha! Shooting stars can never be tamed, my boy. Could you see yourself comfortably settled at home with a shooting star in a cage? Its blinding heat would set fire to the cage and burn you with it, you wouldn't even get close to the bars."

"I don't want to put her in a cage. I just want to give her more confidence."

"Pure alchemy, that's right."

"Put it this way, I was dreaming of a love as great as

Arthur's Seat, and now I find that my bones are growing into a mountain range."

"You're exceptionally lucky, you know, few people ever get near to that feeling."

"Perhaps, but now that I've tasted it, I can't do without it. And when she holds back, I feel so empty."

"Just enjoy the fact that you're experiencing so many emotions. I knew a shooting star once as well, and I can tell you those girls are like mountain weather: unpredictable. Even if Miss Acacia loves you, you'll never be able to master her."

We love each other secretly. Our combined age is no more than thirty. She's the little singing girl, famous since childhood. I'm the outsider who works in the Ghost Train.

The Extraordinarium is like a village, where everybody knows everyone else and gossip travels fast. You get all types of people: jealous, affectionate, moralizing, small-minded, brave, well-intentioned but intrusive.

I'd like to think I'm not the type to worry about what people might say, especially if it means I get to kiss her for a little longer. Miss Acacia, on the other hand, can't abide the idea of anybody finding out about our secret.

This state of affairs suited us rather well to begin with. We felt like pirates, and what kept us going was the magic of stowing away. But when love becomes something greater than its first intense moments, it sets off like a steamboat in a bath. We need space, more and more space . . . Much as we enjoy the moon, we want the sun too.

"I'm going to kiss you in front of everybody," I tell her. "Nothing will happen to us."

"I'd like to kiss you in broad daylight too, and do the things everybody else does. But as long as people can't see us, we're safe from gossip. We'll never live in peace again if someone like Brigitte discovers our secret."

Of course, her sweet words are delicious; I'd happily slip them under my tongue. But I'm finding it harder and harder to watch her disappear into the chinks of the night, as dawn approaches. Her stilettos are like clock hands, beating out a rhythm as she heads off into the distance, triggering my insomnia. When day breaks, my back aches and the birds let me know how short a time I have left to sleep.

In a few months, our love has grown still more. The night is not enough for us. Send us sunlight and fresh air; we need calcium for our growing bones. I don't want to wear the mask of a romantic bat! I want to laugh in the light of day.

Almost a year after we first caught fire, our situation hasn't changed. Nothing more, nothing less. I can't assuage Miss Acacia's fears of what might happen if people find out about us. Méliès tells me to be patient with her. I study the mechanics of her heart passionately. I try opening jammed locks with affectionate keys. But certain places seem closed forever.

Her reputation as an ardent singer has travelled beyond the confines of the Extraordinarium. I enjoy visiting the cabarets in nearby towns to hear her sing; to feel the movement of her flamenco steps. I always arrive after the show has begun, and vanish before it ends, so nobody notices I'm a regular.

After the concerts, crowds of well-dressed men wait in the rain to offer her bouquets of flowers as tall as she is. They court her under my nose. They marvel at the talents of the great little singer, but I have no right to show myself. Here I am on the fringes of her public life, witnessing the eyes of strong-hearted men sparkling in adoration. All this only fans the flames of my passion—and jealousy. The underside of love's medal glints darkly.

This evening, I've decided to try out an experiment to keep her in my bed. I'm going to block my clock hands and stop time. I'll only start the world again if she asks me to. Madeleine forbade me to touch my clock hands but I'm sure it's because she was afraid I would meddle with the passage of time. If Cinderella had owned a clockwork heart, she'd have stopped time at one minute to midnight and stayed at the ball for the rest of her life.

While Miss Acacia slips on her court shoes with one hand and fixes her hair with the other, I block the minute hand.

It has been 4:37 a.m. for a good quarter of an hour, according to my clockwork heart, when I let it go. Meanwhile, Miss Acacia has disappeared into the silent labyrinth of the Extraordinarium, and the first birds of dawn accompany her footsteps.

I wish I had more time to watch her birdlike ankles, to move on up to her streamlined calves, as far as the amber pebbles she has for knees. Then I'd follow her gently open thighs to land on the tenderest of landing strips. There, I'd practice becoming the greatest kisser-caresser in the world. Each time she wanted to go back home, I'd perform my trick. Stopping time, followed by a lesson in languages not foreign. Then, I'd set the world off again, and she'd feel so alive she wouldn't be able to resist spending a few more light-filled minutes in the haven of my bed. For those moments stolen from time, she'd be all mine.

But as perfectly as my old heart measures time, tick-tocking its way through my sleeplessness, it refuses to help me when it comes to magic. I'm sitting here alone on my bed, trying to relieve my aching clock by squeezing the gears between my fingers. *Madeleine, how furious you'd be . . .*

The next morning, I decide to pay Méliès a visit. He's built himself a workshop where he labors at his dream: photography in motion. I drop by to see him nearly every afternoon, before going on to the Ghost Train. I often walk in on him with his *belles.* One day it might be a long-haired brunette, the next a little redhead. But he's still working on his famous voyage to the moon that he wanted to give to the woman of his life.

"As a cure for my own failed love, I indulge in small doses of comfort. It's a gentle medicine that stings a bit sometimes, but it helps me put myself back together again. The magic has turned against me; I told you nothing's guaranteed to work every time. I need to make a full recovery before throwing myself into full-scale emotions again. But don't use me as an example. Carry on soldering your dreams to reality, without forgetting the most important thing: today, Miss Acacia is in love with *you*."

chapter nine

In which a couple of vampires go on a supermarket trip, and fleshy ghosts hang around . . .

Each day, Brigitte Heim threatens to throw me out if I go on making her Ghost Train look comical; but she never makes good her threat, because the customers keep coming in their droves. I do my best to frighten them but I can't help it if I make them laugh instead. No matter how much energy I put into singing "Oh When the Saints" as I limp along like Arthur, or silently smash eggs on my heart under the glow of the candelabra, or playing the violin on my gears to produce creaking melodies, or leaping from carriage to carriage and even onto people's knees for the finale, it's just hopeless: they all burst out laughing. Every single time, I mess up my surprise effects because my tick-tock rings out loud and clear. So the customers know exactly when I'm supposed to scare them, and some regulars even laugh ahead of time. Méliès thinks I'm far too much in love to frighten people properly.

Occasionally, Miss Acacia comes for a ride on the Ghost Train. My clock always tick-tocks more loudly when I see her settling her bird's bottom into a carriage. I slip her a few intimations of ardor, as a precursor to our nocturnal encounters.

Come, my blossoming tree, this evening we'll turn out the light and I'll lay your spectacles to rest on two swelling buds that promise to bring forth leaves. You'll score the celestial vault with the tips of your branches, and shake your invisible trunk as it props up the moon. New dreams will fall back down like warm snow at our feet. You'll plant your high-heeled roots firmly in the earth. Let me climb over your bamboo heart, I want to sleep by your side.

Midnight chimes. I notice a few wood shavings on my bed; my clock is crumbling. Miss Acacia arrives without her glasses, but her eyes look focused as if we were due to have a business meeting.

"You were behaving oddly yesterday evening," she says. "You even let me go without saying goodbye—no kiss, nothing. You were tinkering with your clock, hypnotized. I was frightened you'd cut yourself on those pointy arrows."

"I'm sorry. I just wanted to try out an experiment to make you stay a little longer, but it didn't work."

"No, it didn't. Don't play that game with me. I love you, but you know I can't stay until morning."

"I know, I know . . . that's why I was trying to . . ."

"And while we're on the subject, why don't you take off your clock when we're together? I get bruises from our making—"

"Take off my clock? But I can't!"

"Of course you can! I don't keep my stage makeup on to join you under the sheets, do I?"

"Yes, you do sometimes! And you're very beautiful when you're naked with painted eyes."

A gentle twinkle flashes beneath her eyelashes.

"The point is I could never remove my clock. It's not an accessory."

Her luscious lips pout, as if to say: *I don't even believe seventy percent of what you're saying.*

"You know what, it's great that you believe in your dreams, but you've got to come down off your cloud every once in a while and grow up. You can't go through life with your clock hands sticking out of your coat," she says, sounding like a teacher.

I may be in the same room as her, but not since our first encounter have I been so far away from her embrace.

"Sorry," I tell her, "but yes I can. That really is how I function. This clock is a vital part of me. It's what makes my heart beat. There's no getting away from it. I draw on who I am to overcome my situation, to feel alive. It's just like you onstage; when you sing, it's the same thing."

"It's not the same thing, you naughty boy!" she says, sliding her fingernails over my dial.

That she could even think my clock might just be an "accessory" makes my blood run cold. I couldn't love her if I thought her heart was a fake, whether it was made of glass or flesh or eggshell.

"Well, keep it on if you like, but be careful with your clock hands . . ."

"Do you believe in me one hundred percent?"

"I'd say seventy percent, for the time being. It's up to you to get me all the way to a hundred percent, Little Jack . . ."

"Why am I thirty percent short?"

"Because I know what men are like."

"I'm not like the others."

"Is that what you think?"

"Absolutely."

"You're a born cheat! Even your heart is a cheat."

"The only real thing I have is my heart."

"You see, you always land on your feet. But that's what I love about you."

"I don't want there to be things you 'love about me,' I want you to love 'all of me.'"

Her eyelids are like black parasols, blinking in time to the tick-tock of my heart. Her lips, which I haven't kissed for too long, betray amusement and doubt. The palpitations speed up under my dial. A familiar tingling.

She starts the drumroll as a hint of a dimple lights up her cheeks.

"I love all of you," she concludes.

She places her hands strategically and the wind is taken out of me. My thoughts dissolve into my body. She turns off the light.

Her neck is sprinkled with tiny beauty spots, in a constellation that descends to her breasts. I guess at the astronomy of her skin and bury my nose in her stars. I can't take my eyes off her gently opened mouth. My blood froths and there are sparks flying between my thighs. I graze on her skin and she becomes my flower. A mild electric current flows from her hands. I draw closer.

"To increase my trust ratings, I'm going to give you the key to my heart. You won't be able to remove it, but otherwise you can do whatever you like, whenever you like. You *are* the key that opens up all of me. And since I trust all of you, why don't you put on your glasses and let me see your eyes through those lenses?"

My little singer agrees and pulls her hair back. Her doe's eyes leap out from her elegant face. Then she puts on a pair of Madeleine's glasses and leans her head to one side. Madeleine, how furious you'd be if you could see her!

I'd like to tell Miss Acacia how gorgeous she looks in those glasses, but she wouldn't believe me, so I stroke her hand instead. I start worrying that she might like me less if she could see me as I really am. Now I'm the one who's panicking.

I place the key in her right hand. I'm nervous, which makes me rattle like a toy train.

"Why have you got two holes?"

"The right-hand one is to open me up and the left-hand one to wind me up."

"Can I open you?"

"All right."

She nudges the key delicately into my right keyhole. I close my eyes then open them again, just like when we're kissing for a long time. I want to see everything ablaze.

Her eyelids are closed, magnificently drawn down. It's such a serene moment. She grips a gear between her thumb and index finger, gently, without slowing it down. All of a sudden a tide of tears wells up and overwhelms me. She relaxes her subtle grasp and the waters of melancholy are cut off. Miss Acacia caresses my second gear—will she tickle my heart? I laugh lightly. Then, without letting go of the second gear in her right hand, she returns to the first one with the fingers of her left hand. When she brings her lips to the teeth of my cogs, she works her Blue Fairy magic on me, like in *Pinocchio,* but more real. Except it's not my nose that's growing longer. She senses this and her movements accelerate, increasing the pressure on my gears. Sounds escape from my mouth before I can check myself. I'm surprised, embarrassed, but above all excited. She uses my gears as if they were resistors and my sighs turn to groans.

"I'd like to take a bath," she whispers.

I signal my consent—what is there to disagree with? I land back on my feet so I can head to the bathroom and run a hot bath.

I make my way quietly, not wanting to wake Brigitte.

Her bedroom is on the other side of the wall and we can hear her coughing.

There are silvery reflections: the sky has just fallen into the bathtub. Miraculously, an ordinary tap pours tender stars into the silence of the night. We enter the water gingerly, so as not to splash about in this delight. We are two starry flecks of confectioners' sugar, writ large. And we make the slowest love in the world, with just our tongues. The lapping of the water makes us feel as if each of us is inside the other. I've rarely experienced anything as pleasurable.

We whisper our cries. We have to hold back. Then suddenly she gets up, turns around, and we're transformed into jungle animals.

My whole body collapses; I'm in a western and I've just been shot. She starts groaning slowly. The cuckoo chimes in slow motion. Madeleine . . .

Later, after Miss Acacia has drifted off to sleep, I find myself staring at her. The length of her painted eyelashes emphasizes her ferocious beauty. She's so desirable, I wonder if her singing career hasn't conditioned her to pose for imaginary painters even when she's fast asleep. She looks like a Modigliani painting—a Modigliani that snores just a tiny bit.

Her life as a little singer with a burgeoning career continues; with its admirers who hang around her with no particular purpose, like fleshy ghosts.

All those perfumed human bodies frighten me more than a pack of wolves beneath a full moon. It's all fake, and the chitchat is as hollow as a funeral vault. I think how brave she is to swim over this eddy of make-believe.

One day, they'll send her to the moon to test out how aliens react to such an erotic display. She'll sing and dance and answer local journalists' questions; then they'll take her photo and she'll never come back. Sometimes I think all that's missing is Joe: the worm-eaten cherry on top of the rotten cake.

A week later, Miss Acacia is singing in Seville. I ride my roller-board over the red mountains to catch up with her in her hotel bedroom after the show.

Along the way, the carrier pigeon drops off a new letter from Madeleine. Did my previous letter not get to her? Her note is only a few words long, and, worse, they're words that don't seem to be hers. They leave me wanting more . . . I'd give anything for Madeleine to meet Miss Acacia. Of course, our love would frighten her, but she couldn't help liking my little singer's personality. Imagining these two she-wolves talking together is a dream that always soothes me.

The day after the concert, we're walking around Seville like proper lovers. The temperature's just right and a warm wind strokes our skin. Our fingers fumble when it comes to doing the things that normal people do in broad daylight. At night, remote-controlled by desire, they know each other intricately; but for now, they are like four left hands being asked to write "hello."

How clumsy we are from head to toe. Like a couple of vampires who've forgotten their sunglasses, out on a supermarket trip. But it's a romantic dream for us. And kissing on the banks of the river Guadalquivir, in the middle of the afternoon, is a complete turn-on.

Above this sweet and simple happiness hovers a menacing cloud. I'm proud of Miss Acacia as I've never been proud before in my life. But the ecstatic looks from other men are making me feel increasingly jealous. I try persuading myself that, since she's not wearing her spectacles, she might not be able to see this herd of men more handsome than me. But when the ever-expanding crowds rise to applaud, I feel alone in their midst; it's time to play the role of the outsider and head back home to my shadowy attic.

Her refusal to acknowledge my suffering only makes things worse. I still don't think she really believes in my cuckoo-clock heart.

I haven't yet explained to her that behaving the way I do, with a makeshift heart, is as dangerous as a diabetic eating chocolate éclairs from morning till night. I'm not sure I want to explain this to her, either. If Madeleine's theories are to be believed, I'm knocking on death's door.

Will I be able to rise to the occasion? Will my old ticker hold out?

To spice up an already fiery sauce, Miss Acacia is at least as jealous as I am. She frowns like a lioness ready to pounce the moment any kid-girl, who's bothered to brush her hair, enters my field of vision; even outside the Ghost Train.

I was flattered at first and able to rise above such obstacles. My wings were new. I was sure she believed in me. But when I found out she thought I was a cheat, I felt more vulnerable. In the depths of my nocturnal solitude, I've stopped believing in myself.

That fiery sauce is threatening to turn into hedgehog soup.

chapter ten

In which a walking lamppost crosses half of Europe

One day, a peculiar man heads for the Ghost Train, his sights firmly set on my job of Scareperson. That's when the hedgehog soup gets stuck in my throat.

He's tall, very tall. His head appears to tower over the roof of the Ghost Train. His right eye is masked by a black patch. His left eye scrutinizes the Extraordinarium like a lighthouse casting its beam over the sea. It finally comes to rest on the figure of Miss Acacia. And stays there.

Brigitte, who despairs of ever seeing me pull off a show based on fear, hires him on the spot. I'm kicked out. It all happens much too quickly for my liking. I'll have to ask

Méliès to put me up in his workshop. I don't know how the precious intimacy I share with the little singer will survive such conditions.

That evening, Miss Acacia is singing in a theater in town. As usual, I slip in to the back of the auditorium after the first song. The new Scareperson is sitting in the first row. He's so tall that he's blocking half the audience's view. At any rate, I can't see a thing.

This new eye fixed on Miss Acacia makes me stew in my shirt. The man doesn't turn off his revolving light once during the entire evening, not even after the concert is over. I'd like to tell him to get lost, that great big walking lamppost. But I hold back. My heart, on the other hand, doesn't waste any time shouting itself hoarse, singing *la* in a minor key and decidedly out of tune. The whole auditorium turns round to laugh. Some of the audience members ask how I produce such strange noises, then one of them calls out:

"I recognize you! You're the guy who makes everybody laugh on the Ghost Train!"

"As of yesterday, I don't work there anymore."

"Ah, sorry . . . I liked your gag, it was very funny."

I could be back in the school playground. All the confidence I've gained in Miss Acacia's arms has taken flight. I'm being slowly dismantled.

After the show, it's hard not to open up to my chosen one, who retorts:

"That great oaf? Pahhh . . ."

"He looks hypnotized by you."

"You're the one who's always talking about trust, and now you're kicking up a fuss about that one-eyed pirate over there?"

"I'm not blaming you. I can see that he's the one who's circling you like a shark."

The ground's gone from under my feet. Much as I trust her, I've no doubt this pirate will do everything in his power to seduce her. There's no mistaking certain looks, even those cast by a single eye. In fact that only makes it worse, because the intensity is doubled.

But just when the hedgehog soup gets too fiery to swallow, the great one-eyed oaf comes over to us and says:

"Don't you recognize me?"

As he utters these words, a long shudder runs down my spine. It's a familiar feeling, one I haven't experienced since school, and I detest it.

"Joe! What on earth are you doing here?" Miss Acacia exclaims, embarrassed.

"I've been on a long journey to find you, both of you, a very long journey . . ."

His diction is slow and deliberate. Apart from the eye and a few wispy bits of beard, he hasn't changed. It's odd I didn't recognize him straightaway. I'm finding it hard to register that Joe is here in person. In an attempt to remain cheerful, I keep repeating to myself: *This isn't the right backdrop for you, Joe, go back to your Scottish mists, right now!*

"Do you two know each other?" asks Miss Acacia.

"We went to school together. We're—how can I put it—old acquaintances," he answers, with a smile.

The hatred I feel toward Joe paralyzes me. I'd happily put out his second eye on the spot, if it would send him back to where he's come from, but I'm trying to keep my cool in front of my little singer.

"We need to talk," he tells me, fixing me with his cold eye.

"Midday tomorrow, in front of the Ghost Train, just the two of us."

"All right. And don't forget to bring your spare set of keys," he replies.

Sure enough, that same evening Joe takes up his quarters in what used to be my bedroom. He'll be sleeping in the bed where Miss Acacia and I first made love, walking down corridors where we so often kissed, catching glimpses of our dreams in mirrors . . . Hidden in the bathroom, we can hear him unpacking his things.

"Joe's one of your ex-lovers, isn't he?"

"Oh come off it, a lover? I was a child at the time. When I see him now, I wonder what on earth I saw in a boy like him!"

"I'm wondering exactly the same thing . . . In fact, I'm asking you."

"He was the big shot at school, everybody was in awe of him. I was very young, end of story. Isn't it a funny coincidence that we both know him!"

"Not really, no."

I don't want to tell her the story about the eye. I'm worried she'll think I'm some kind of dangerous lunatic. I can feel the trap closing in on me. I'm paranoid about Joe's comeback and I don't know how to handle this situation.

"Why did he ask for the spare set of keys?"

"Brigitte Heim has just hired him, instead of me, for the Ghost Train. And as of this evening, he's also taking my bedroom."

"That woman doesn't understand a thing."

"The problem is Joe."

"She'd have kicked you out anyway. We'll find a different hiding place, come on . . . We'll spend our nights in the cemetery if we have to. At least that way you can pretend to give me real flowers. Look, don't worry about it, you'll find a job somewhere else in no time. You might not have to frighten people anymore for a living. I'm sure if you concentrate on what you're good at, you'll find something much better than the Ghost Train. And stop making such a big deal out of Joe's return. You're the only one I want, you do realize that?"

Her words catch fire inside me, but then go out. Panic weaves a spider's web in my throat, ensnaring my voice. I'd like to put on a brave face, but I'm cracking all over the place. Come on, old drum, stand up to the test.

I try restarting my clockwork heart, but it's no good, I just sink deeper into the Scottish gloom of my childhood memories. Fear gets the upper hand, just like when I was at school. Madeleine, how furious you'd be . . . I wish you could whisper *"love is dangerous for your tiny heart"* into my ear this evening. I need you so badly right now . . .

．　．　．

The sun beats down on the Ghost Train roof. It's exactly midday, going by the clock in my heart. My fair skin burns gently while I'm waiting for Joe. Three birds of prey circle silently.

He's here for vengeance. Stealing Miss Acacia from me would be the perfect payback. The Alhambra's arches swallow their own shadows. A drop of salty sweat forms on my forehead, trickles into my right eye and sets off a tear.

Joe appears at the corner of the main avenue that runs through the Extraordinarium. I'm quivering, more with rage than fear. I try to look casual, even though my gears are burning under my skin. My heart's palpitations are noisier than a gravedigger's shovel.

Joe stops ten meters away, standing straight across from me. His shadow licks the dust off his footprints.

"I wanted to see you again, and it's not just to get my revenge, whatever you might think . . ."

His voice is still a weapon to be reckoned with. Like Brigitte Heim's, it has the gift of smashing the windows of my dreams.

"I'm not thinking anything. You humiliated and bullied me for years. One day, all that turned against you. As far as I'm concerned, we're quits."

"I admit I hurt you by cutting you off from everyone at school. I only realized how much you'd suffered afterward, when I was left with one eye. I saw the scared looks. I felt people changing how they behaved toward me. You'd think I was contagious, the way some of them avoided me, and that by talking to me they risked losing their own eyes. Each day, I understood more about how damaged I must have left you feeling . . ."

"I don't suppose you've crossed half of Europe to say you're sorry."

"No, you're right. We still have a few scores to settle. Didn't you ever wonder why I gave you such a hard time?"

"Yes, at the beginning . . . I even tried talking to you, but you were a brick wall. I was living in that house, remember, the one belonging to the *witch who delivers children from prostitutes' bellies.'* And, as you never stopped reminding me, I probably *'came out of a prostitute's belly too'* . . . I was new, the smallest kid in the class, and my heart made odd noises. It was easy to make fun of me, to tower above me physically. I was your ideal victim. Until that dreadful day when you took it too far."

"Yes, that's part of the story. But the main reason I picked on you was that on the first day of school, you asked me if I knew somebody you referred to as 'the little singer.' As far as I was concerned, you'd just signed your own death warrant. I was head over heels in love. I'd spent the whole school year before you turned up trying to get close to Miss Acacia, without success. But one spring day, while she was skating on the frozen river and practicing her singing as she liked to do, the ice cracked under her feet. I managed to rescue her with my long legs and big arms. She could have died. I can still picture her shivering as I held her. We were inseparable from that day on until the beginning of summer. I'd never felt so happy. But on the first day of the autumn term, after dreaming all holidays about being reunited with her, I found out that she'd stayed in Granada, and nobody knew when she'd be back."

Coming from Joe's mouth, the word "dreaming" sounds as incongruous as an Alsatian dog being careful not to get any crumbs on his coat while he eats a croissant.

"And that same day you show up like a leprechaun with a satchel, and tell me you want to meet her so you can give her a pair of spectacles! Missing her was bad enough, but you made me feel even more jealous by revealing the terrible thing we had in common. It's what still links us today: our boundless love for Miss Acacia. I remember the noise your heart used to make when you were talking about her. I despised you on the spot. That tick-tock measured the time slipping away without her. Your clock was a torture instrument filled with your own dreams of love for *my* Miss Acacia."

"That doesn't justify the way you humiliated me every single day. How could I know what had gone on before?"

"Fine. But just because I humiliated you, it didn't warrant THIS!"

He lifts his bandage abruptly. His eye is a sort of egg white, sullied by blood and worm-eaten with gray-blue varicose veins.

"I told you," he goes on, "this handicap taught me a great

deal about myself and about life in general. As far as you and I are concerned, I agree, we're quits."

He finds it insanely difficult to get this last sentence out. And I find it insanely difficult to listen.

"We *were* quits," I answer. "But by coming here, you're picking on me again."

"I haven't come here to get my revenge, I've told you that. I've come to take Miss Acacia back to Edinburgh. I've been chewing this moment over for years. Even while I was kissing other girls. Your bloody tick-tock has been so loud inside my head, you as good as infected me with your disease the day you poked my eye out. If she doesn't want me, I'll leave. But if it's the other way around, you'll have to disappear. I don't hold a grudge against you anymore, but I'm still in love with her."

"I've still got plenty of grudges against you."

"Well, get used to it, because I'm worthy of Miss Acacia too. It'll be an old-fashioned contest, and she's the only judge. May the best man win, Little Jack."

He smiles that smug smile I'm all too familiar with as he extends his long fingers. I hand over my bedroom keys. I have the sickening feeling that I'm offering him the keys to Miss Acacia's heart. And I realize that the magical entertainment with my bespectacled fire-girl is over.

What about our dream of a beachfront cabin where we'd be able to walk in peace night and day? Her skin, her smile, her repartee, her sparkling character all made me want to have children with her. But that was yesterday.

Now Joe has come to fetch her. I'm foundering in the haze of my oldest demons. My clock arrows shrivel inside their fragile dial. I'm not done yet, but I'm frightened, very frightened.

Instead of watching Miss Acacia's belly grow, like a happy gardener taking stock, I have to get the armor out of the wardrobe and face Joe one more time.

That evening, Miss Acacia shows up at my bedroom door, her eyes flashing angrily. I'm trying to close my messily packed suitcase, and sense that the next few minutes are going to be stormy.

"Watch out, mountain weather ahead!" I joke, trying to calm things down between us.

If her balmy sweetness knows no match, this evening my little singer is the opposite. She spits lightning.

"So, just like that, you poke someone's eye out! Who on earth have I fallen in love with?"

"I . . ."

"How could you have done anything so hideous? You-poked-his-eye-out!"

Baptism by fire, a flamenco tornado with gunpowder castanets and stilettos digging into my nerves. I wasn't expecting this. I'm searching for something to say, but she doesn't give me time.

"Who are you *really*? And if you hid something as serious as that from me, what else will I find out about?"

Her eyes are dilated with anger, but even more unbearable is the genuine sadness that frames them.

"How could you have hidden something so monstrous from me?" she says again and again.

That bastard Joe has just lit the darkest fuse by digging up my past. I don't want to lie to my little singer. But I don't want to tell her everything either, which I guess amounts to a half-lie.

"All right, so I poked one of his eyes out. Of course I'd much rather it'd never come to that, but what he didn't tell you was how *he* made my life miserable for years; and, more importantly, *why* . . . Thanks to Joe, I experienced the blackest hours of my life. At school, I was his favorite victim. Picture it. A new boy, a pipsqueak, whose heart makes strange noises . . . Joe spent his time humiliating me, making me feel how different I was from everyone else. I was a toy for him. One day he smashed an egg on my head, the next day he dented my clock, every day something new, and always in public."

"I know he likes to brag. He craves attention. But he's never really cruel. I'm sure he didn't give you any reason to behave like a criminal."

"I didn't poke his eye out because he was bragging. The problem goes back much further than that."

My memories come through in waves and my words are having a hard time riding them. I'm ashamed and saddened. I do my best to express myself calmly.

"It all started the day before my tenth birthday. It was my first time in town, I can remember it like it was yesterday. I heard you singing, then I saw you. My clock hands pointed toward you, as if attracted to a magnetic field. My cuckoo started singing. Madeleine was restraining me. I escaped her grip to go and stand right in front of you. The way I sang the response, you'd think we were in some outlandish musical comedy. You sang, I answered, we were communicating in a language I didn't know, but we understood each other perfectly. You danced and I danced with you, even though I had no idea how to dance. Anything felt possible."

"I remember, right from the very beginning I remembered. The moment I found you in my dressing room, I knew it was you." The sadness doesn't leave her voice. "That strange little boy from when I was ten years old, the one who slumbered at the back of my memories. I was sure it was you . . ."

"You remember . . . D'you remember what a bubble we were in? It took Madeleine's fist to burst it."

"I stepped on my glasses and when I put them on my nose, they were all bent."

"Yes! Glasses with a bandage on the right lens. Madeleine said it was to make the weak eye work harder."

"She was right . . ."

"From that day on, I never stopped dreaming of finding you again. When I discovered where you went to school, I begged Madeleine to let me enroll. I waited for so long, but instead of you I got Joe. Joe and his stooges. On my first day at school, I had the misfortune to ask if anybody knew *the beautiful little singer who's always bumping into things.* Joe couldn't bear the fact that you were no longer by his side, so he took all his frustration out on me. He could tell how crazy I was about you, which made him even more jealous. Every morning I walked through the school gates with a knot of panic that stayed in the pit of my stomach for the rest of the day. I endured his attacks at school for three years. Until the day he decided to tear off my shirt, so I was bare-chested in front of the whole school. He wanted to open up my clock and humiliate me even more, but I'd had enough of being pushed around. We got into a fight and it ended badly, very badly, as you know. So I left Edinburgh in the middle of the night, headed for Andalusia. I crossed half of Europe in search of you. It wasn't always easy. I missed Madeleine, Arthur, Anna and Luna, I still miss them . . . But my greatest dream was to see you again. And now, Joe is back to snatch that dream. He'll do everything in his power to turn you away from me. He's already begun, can't you see?"

"Do you really think I'd get back together with him?"

"Look, I don't doubt you, but what if he destroys the trust we've built up piece by piece? I hardly recognize you since he turned up. He's taken my place on the Ghost Train, he sleeps in our bed, which used to be the only place where we were safe from the outside world. As soon as I turn my back, he spreads gossip about my past . . . I feel as if I've been stripped of everything."

"But you . . ."

"Listen to me. One day, he looked me straight in the eye and warned me: *I'll smash that wooden heart on your head, I'll smash it so hard you'll never be able to love again.* He knows where to aim."

"You too, or so it would seem."

"Why do you think he decided to tell you his version of the story about his poked-out eye?"

She shrugs, like a sad bird.

"Joe knows how uncompromising you are. He knows how to set fire to the strands of your hair, which connect to your heart grenade. You do a very good impression of a bomb, but he also knows how vulnerable you are underneath. He knows that if he introduces an element of doubt, you might implode. Joe is trying to wear us down so that he can win you back. If you'd only realize that, you could help me stop him."

She turns toward me, slowly raising her parasol-eyelids. Two fat tears trickle down her magnificent face. Her makeup runs over her crumpled eyelashes. She has a strange talent for looking as captivating in suffering as in joy.

"I love you."

"I love you too."

I kiss her tear-filled mouth. She tastes of overripe fruit. Then Miss Acacia walks away. I watch the forest wrap itself around her, as the shadowy branches gobble her up.

In a few steps she's vanished. Oh Madeleine, this tempo of shattering dreams makes my gears get noisier, and more painful too. I've got this horrible feeling Miss Acacia and I will never see each other again.

chapter eleven

In which our hero asks, "Oh Madeleine, where are you when I need you most?"

On the way to Méliès's workshop, my clock rattles alarmingly. The Alhambra's bewitching alcoves echo back.

When I get there, nobody's in. I sit down in the middle of all those cardboard cutouts. Lost among so many inventions, I become one of them. I'm a human gimmick, who wishes he could ditch the special effects. At my age, the only "effect" I'd like to have on people is being thought of as a proper grown-up man. But have I got the talent to show Miss Acacia what I'm made of, and how much I burn for her? Can she believe in me, or will she always think I'm playing some sort of trick on her?

My dreams stretch to the top of Arthur's Seat. I'd like to teleport that mountain here, in front of the Alhambra. To find out what's happened to my makeshift family. I'd give anything for them to appear here, right now. I miss them so badly . . .

Madeleine and Méliès would talk about psychology and "tinkering with things," over a delicious meal cooked from one of my midwife-mother's secret recipes. She and Miss Acacia would spark each other off on the subject of love; they'd probably tear each other's hair out too. But all hostilities would cease with the aperitif. They'd tease each other, acerbic one moment, kind the next, until they were in cahoots at last. And then Anna, Luna and Arthur would join us, peppering the discussion with tales by turns tragic and outlandish.

"What's with the sad face . . . ?" enquires Méliès, pushing open the door.

"Come on, little one, let me show you my *belles*!"

The pretty girls keeping him company are a tall giggly blonde, and a plump brunette who drags on her cigarette holder like it's an oxygen bottle.

"Ladies, this is my travelling companion," Méliès introduces me, "my most loyal ally, and the friend who saved me from a broken heart."

I'm touched. The girls applaud as they bat their tantalizing eyelashes.

"Sorry," Méliès adds for my benefit, "but I have to retire

to my bedchamber for a restorative siesta that may last a few centuries."

"And your voyage to the moon?"

"Everything in its own time, don't you think? We have to learn to 'unwind' every so often. Lying low is all part of the creative process!"

I'd like to talk to him about Joe, to have him look at the state of my gears, to ask him more questions about living with a shooting star, but it's clearly not the right moment. His birds are already clucking in boiling water, shrouded in cigarette smoke. I'd better leave him to enjoy his sensual bath.

"Miss Acacia might come by to see me tonight, if that's all right with you . . ."

"Of course it is, this is your home too."

I return to the Ghost Train to pick up the rest of my belongings. The thought of leaving this place for good is another blow to my clock. The Ghost Train is haunted by wonderful memories of Miss Acacia. I was even starting to enjoy the way people found my performances funny.

A large poster featuring Joe has been stuck up over mine. The bedroom is locked. The belongings I couldn't squeeze into my suitcase are waiting for me in the corridor, piled up on my roller-board. I've turned into a bloody ghost! I'm still useless at frightening anyone, nobody laughs when I pass by, nobody sees me. I'm invisible, even to Brigitte Heim's pragmatic gaze. It's as if I no longer exist.

A boy calls out from the queue.

"Excuse me, Señor, but aren't you the clock-man?"

"Who, me?"

"Yes, you! I recognize that noise your heart makes. So . . . are you coming back to the Ghost Train?"

"No, I'm just leaving, as it happens."

"But you've got to come back, Señor! It's not the same without you . . ."

I wasn't expecting this; something starts vibrating under my gears.

"I kissed a girl for the first time on this Ghost Train, you see. But she won't set foot here anymore, now we've got Big Joe. She's scared. Don't leave us to Big Joe, sir!"

"Yes, we used to have fun here!" calls out a second kid.

"Come back," another follows up.

While I'm greeting this small gathering and thanking them for their warm words, my cuckoo starts up. Three of the boys clap and a few adults join in timidly.

I climb onto my roller-board and head down the main avenue that flanks the Alhambra, cheered on by a section of the crowd:

"Come back! Come back!"

All of a sudden, a deep gravelly voice booms: "Go away!"

I turn around. Behind me, Joe flashes his winner's smile. If a Tyrannosaurus could produce a grin, it would look like Joe's. Rare and terrifying.

"I'm just leaving, but I'm warning you, I'll be back. You've won the battle for the Ghost Train, but I'm king of the heart that belongs to *you-know-who.*"

The crowd starts to egg us on, like at a cockfight.

"So, you haven't noticed anything?"

"What?"

"You don't think Miss Acacia's behavior has changed toward you?"

"Let's settle this matter in private, Joe. Don't mention names in public."

"You're the ones I heard arguing in the bathroom last night . . ."

"Because you're trying to make her believe terrible things about me."

"I simply told her you punched my eye out for no reason. That's fair enough, isn't it?"

One part of the queue is leaning toward Joe; the other, in the minority, is on my side.

"You said an old-fashioned contest, good and clean. Liar!"

"What about you? You're dreaming your life away, trying to turn everything into a special effect, and those romantic inventions of yours are just bullshit. Your style may be different, but it all comes down to the same thing in the end . . . So anyway, have you seen her today?"

"No, not yet."

"I've taken your job, I've taken your bedroom, and you've lost everything. Admit it, Little Jack, you've lost her. Yesterday, after your fight, she came knocking on my bedroom door. She wanted to be comforted, because of that jealous fit you'd had . . . I didn't talk to her about your ridiculous clock business. I talked to her about the real things that matter to everybody. Was she planning to set-tle down in the area, what sort of house would she like to live in, did she want children, that kind of thing, do you see?"

A shot of doubt. My spine is shaking like a bell. I can hear everything shuddering inside me.

"And we recalled the day she nearly got trapped in the frozen lake. She buried herself in my arms at that point. Just like before, exactly like before."

"I'll punch your other eye out, you scumbag!"

"And we kissed. Just like before, exactly like before."

My head is spinning, I'm losing my grip. Far away, I can hear Brigitte Heim starting to harangue the crowd. The train ride is about to begin. My heart is choking me. I must look as ugly as a condemned man smoking his last cigar.

Before heading off for his performance, Joe taunts me one last time:

"You didn't even notice you were losing everything. I thought I'd be dealing with a tougher opponent. You really don't deserve her."

I charge at him, my clock hands sticking out. I feel like a miniature bull with plastic horns, and Joe's the smiling matador preparing to deal the death blow. Effortlessly, he grabs me by the collar with his right hand and sends me sprawling in the dust.

Then he disappears inside the Ghost Train, followed by the crowd. I stay there for what seems an eternity, my left arm propped against my roller-board, unable to react.

.   .   .

I make it back to Méliès's workshop in the end. But it takes forever. Each time my minute hand jerks, a knife is being thrust deeper between my bones.

It's midnight by my heart's clock. While I'm waiting for Miss Acacia, I stare at the cardboard moon my romantic conjurer has made for his sweetheart. Ten past midnight, twenty-five past, twenty to one. Nobody. My clockwork heart is heating up, there's trouble brewing. That hedgehog soup is getting fierier, even though I've tried not to season it with too many doubts.

Méliès comes out of his bedroom, followed by his jovial retinue of buttocks and bosoms. Even when he's over the moon, he can spot if I'm down in the dumps. With an affectionate glance, he signals to his *belles* to tone it down, so their cheeriness doesn't make me feel any more miserable.

But she doesn't come.

chapter twelve

In which Miss Acacia is attacked by floorboard crocodiles in Granada

The next day, Miss Acacia is giving a concert at a cabaret in the coastal resort of Marbella, a hundred kilometers from Granada. "It's the perfect opportunity to meet up with her again, away from Joe," Méliès tells me.

He lends me his best suit and his favorite hat. Feverishly, I ask him to go with me; he agrees, just as he did on the first day.

Fear and doubt jostle with desire as we set off. Why is it so complicated to keep the person you love close to you? Miss Acacia gives without counting the cost; there's nothing mean-spirited about her. And although I try to return this generosity, she receives less from me. Perhaps I don't know how to give properly. But I refuse to be kicked off the most magical train ride of my life, complete with an engine that spits flaming daffodil petals. Tonight, I'll explain to her that I'm ready to change in every way, provided she loves me. And then things can go back to the way they used to be.

The show is to take place on a tiny stage set along the seashore. Yet the whole world appears to be gathered around it. In the front row sits Joe. A totem invested with powers to make my entire body tremble.

My little singer walks onstage, clicking her heels with a violence that surprises the audience, louder and louder. She shouts, screeches, deals blows with her cries. Today she's inhabited by a wolf. A gutsy blues weaves in and out of her flamenco. Chili peppers dance on her tongue. In her sparkling orange dress, she looks like a singing powder keg. She's got so much tension to exorcise this evening.

All of a sudden, her left leg punctures the floorboard, then her right leg, in a fiery fracas. I rush to help her, but the crowd won't let me through. People just stand there and shout as she hammers herself in like a living nail. My eyes meet hers, I don't think she even recognizes me—perhaps because of Méliès's hat. Joe rushes toward her, his long legs slicing efficiently through the crowd. I'm struggling in his wake. He's gaining ground. In a few seconds, he'll be able to touch her. I can't let her inside those arms of his. Miss Acacia's face tenses, she must be injured. She's not the kind to complain for no reason. I wish I were a doctor or, better still, a sorcerer able to pop her back on her feet. I clamber over the roof of the crowd, walking over people's heads as if I were back on the Ghost Train. I'm going to catch up with him, I'm going to catch up with her. She's hurt herself, I can't bear for her to be in pain. People are pressing against the stage now, keen to "see what's going on." I'm level with Joe, I'm going to stop those floor-board crocodiles from gobbling her up. It'll be me this time. I'll rescue Miss Acacia, and in doing so I'll rescue myself.

From the bottom of my gears a pain shoots across my lungs. Joe has overtaken me. In slow motion, his long fingers scoop up Miss Acacia. I got carried away with my dream of saving her. He covers her bird's body. My clock screeches like a thousand chalks across a board. He lifts up Miss Acacia like a newlywed. She looks so beautiful, even in his arms. They disappear into the dressing room. I try not to shout, I tremble instead. Help, Madeleine! Send me an army of steely hearts.

I've got to break this door down. I smash my head against it. The door doesn't budge. I pick up my body and some of my mind from the floor. I notice my reflection in the pane. A bluish bump has sprung up on my left temple.

After several attempts the door opens, to reveal Miss Acacia lying in Joe's arms. Her red dress, gently pulled up, matches the drops of blood forming on her calves. You'd think he'd just taken a bite out of her and was getting ready to eat her alive.

"Whatever happened to you?" she asks, reaching out to stroke the bump on my head.

I dodge her.

My heart detects the affection in her movement, but can't process it yet. My anger is still raging. Miss Acacia's eyes harden. Joe holds her little bird's body tight to his powerful chest, protecting her from me. Oh Madeleine, your slate must be trembling above my bed. The clock is pounding under my tongue.

Miss Acacia asks Joe to go outside. He does so with the old-fashioned politeness of a judo master. But before exiting, he gently puts Miss Acacia down on a chair; he's clearly frightened she might break. His solicitous gestures are unbearable.

"Did you kiss Joe?"

"Sorry?"

"You did!"

I've set off an avalanche.

"How could you even think such a thing? He just helped me free my leg from that rotten plank. You saw what happened, didn't you?"

"Yes, but yesterday, he . . ."

"Do you honestly believe I want to get back together with him? Do you really think I could do that to you? You don't understand anything!"

Fear of losing her and a raging headache come together

in an electric storm; I'm out of control. I'm about to vomit glowing embers. I can feel them rising up in my throat, invading my brain. My head is short-circuiting. I say dreadful things, sentences I'll never be able to retract.

I wish I could roll those words back up with my tongue, but the venom is already taking effect. The bonds between us are snapping, one by one. I'm sinking our boat, smashing it with cruel accusations. I have to stop this machine that spits resentment before it's too late, but I can't.

Joe opens the door quietly. He doesn't say a word, just sticks his head round, to show Miss Acacia he's keeping an eye on her.

"Everything's fine, Joe. Don't worry."

Her pupils glow with infinite sadness, but her pretty mouth betrays anger and disdain. I used to watch those eyelashes blossoming: now they give off blind fog.

The only advantage of this coldest of showers is to put me back in touch with reality. I'm destroying everything, I can see it in the shattered mirror of her gaze; I've got to turn the clock back, and fast.

I give everything I've got, opening the floodgates wide on to what I've always hidden from her. I should have started with this, I know, I'm doing it all the wrong way round, but I'm still trying to change tack, even now.

"I love you crookedly because my heart's been unhinged from birth. The doctors gave me strict instructions not to fall in love: my fragile clockwork heart would never survive. But when you gave me a dose of love so powerful—far beyond my wildest dreams—that I felt able to confront anything for you, I decided to put my life in your hands."

No sign of a dimple on her cheeks.

"I'm doing everything back to front today because I don't know how to stop losing you and it's making me sick. I love yo—"

"The worst is you actually believe your lies!" she cuts me off. "It's pathetic. There's no way you'd be behaving like this if there was a grain of truth in what you're saying . . . No way. Get out, get out, please!"

The short-circuiting intensifies, spreading to my clock which glows red. Mournful screeching as the gears crash against each other. My brain is on fire, and my heart is rising up into my head. Surely the person with the controls can see this, by looking into my eyes.

"So I'm a fraud, am I? A con artist? Well, let's see about that, shall we, why waste any time?"

I wrench my clock hands as hard as I can. It's horrifically painful. I grab hold of the dial with both hands and, like a person deranged, try ripping out the clock. I want her to see me banishing this millstone and throwing it in the bin, so she understands. The pain is intolerable. First jolt. Nothing happens. Second, still nothing. The third, more violent, feels like knife blows raining down on me. Far away, I can hear her voice calling out: *"stop it . . . stop it!"* But it's too late, a bulldozer is smashing everything between my lungs.

·   ·   ·

Some people claim to see intense light as death approaches. I only saw shadows. Giant shadows as far as the horizon. And a storm of black snowflakes; black snow progressively covering my hands, then my outstretched arms. The dressing table is so drenched in blood that red roses appear to be growing out of it. Then the roses vanish, and my body with them. I'm relaxed and anxious at the same time, as if getting ready for a long-haul flight.

A last spray of sparks flashes up on the screen of my eyelids: Miss Acacia dancing, poised on those stilettos spindly as clock hands, Dr. Madeleine leaning over me, winding up my clockwork heart, Arthur roaring his swing to the beat of "Oh When the Saints," Miss Acacia dancing on clock hands, Miss Acacia dancing on clock hands, Miss Acacia dancing on clock hands . . .

The terrified screams of Miss Acacia finally rouse me from my trance. I raise my head and look up at her. I've got two broken clock hands in my palms. The sadness and anger in her gaze have given way to fear. Her cheeks are hollow; her eyebrows punctuate her forehead like two circumflex accents. Yesterday her eyes were filled with love; today they're leaky cauldrons. I feel as though I'm being stared at by a pretty corpse. A sense of shame overwhelms me, as the rage I feel toward myself outstrips even the fury Joe provokes in me.

·   ·   ·

Miss Acacia walks out of her dressing room. The door slams like a gunshot. A bird shakes itself on my hat; Méliès must have forgotten to remove it. I'm feeling cold, so cold. This has to be the coldest night on earth. I'd be more relaxed if somebody was knitting my heart with icy pokers.

She walks past me without looking back, and disappears into the dark like a sad comet. I hear the sound of her bumping into a lamppost, followed by swearing in Spanish. My brain orders up a smile from my memories, but the message gets lost along the way.

A few meters above the stage, lightning rips across the sky. Umbrellas open like funeral flowers; I'm rather tired of dying all the time.

I hold my clock in place with the flat of my hand. Blood on the gears. My head is spinning, I don't know how to make my legs work anymore. When I try walking, I'm as knock-kneed as a first-time skier.

My cuckoo coughs with each of my spasms, leaving wood chippings all around. Heavy sleep overcomes me. I melt into the mist with Jack the Ripper on my mind. Will I end up like him, only successful in relationships with dead women?

Everything I did, I did for Miss Acacia. But my dreams—and my reality—haven't worked out. I wanted it to work, wanted it so badly, probably too much. I thought I could do anything for her, crumbling the moon to make her eyelids sparkle; never sleeping before the sound of birds yawning at dawn; going to the ends of the earth to find her . . . Is this what it's all come to?

A flash of lightning slaloms between the trees, ending its journey in silence on the beach. The sea lights up for a moment. Perhaps Miss Acacia still has something to say to me?

Then the foam retreats and Marbella switches back into darkness. The spectators bolt from the rain like rabbits into a warren. It's time for me to pack up my suitcase of dreams.

chapter thirteen

In which Little Jack has a change of heart and a gigantic hangover

It takes Méliès two days to drag my carcass from Marbella back to Granada. When we finally reach the city's outskirts, the Alhambra looms like an elephants' graveyard. Its fortifications glint in the darkness, ready to butcher me.

"Get up! Get up!" whispers Méliès, "don't give in, don't leave me!"

Everything's coming apart inside me. I squint over the stumps of my clock hands. It's a terrifying sight that reminds me of when I was born.

Nothing makes sense anymore. As a newly fledged adult, I used to want to look after my clock, so I would last long enough to realize my dream of having a family of my own: but all that has dissolved like snowflakes in the flames. What rose-tinted nonsense love is! Madeleine had warned me, of course, but I wanted to follow my heart.

I'm dragging myself along with painstaking slowness. A huge fire rages inside my chest, but I feel anesthetized. I wouldn't notice if an airplane flew straight between my eyes.

I'd give anything to see Arthur's Seat rise up before me. Oh Madeleine, if only! I'd dive straight into my bed. There must be a few childhood dreams still hidden under my pillow. I'd do my best not to crush them, heavy though my head is with grown-up worries. I'd go to sleep thinking I'd never wake up again; which is a strangely comforting idea. The next morning I'd have a hard time coming to, knocked out like a failed boxer. But Madeleine would lavish her attentions on me, restoring me to how I was before. Just because a letter never came doesn't stop me from talking to my midwife-mother in my head . . .

Back in his workshop, Méliès tucks me up in his bed. Blood spreads across the white sheets. Snow-roses reappearing, twirling. *Bloody hell, I'm staining the sheets,* I think in a flash of consciousness. My head weighs a ton, and my brain is as tired of being trapped inside my head as my heart is under my clock dial.

"I want to change my heart. Make me different, I don't

want to be me anymore. Don't you see, I've had enough of this wooden heart; it's like a dead weight that keeps cracking all the time."

Méliès watches over me, concerned.

"Your problem goes much deeper than your wooden clock, you know."

"I feel as if a giant acacia tree is growing between my lungs. This evening, *I saw* Joe carrying Miss Acacia in his arms and it was like being stabbed. I'd never have believed it could be so hard. And when she slammed the door and left, it was harder still."

"You knew the risks, my boy, when you gave a shooting star the keys to your heart."

"I want you to fit me with a new heart and set the counter back to zero. I never want to fall in love again."

Noticing the mad suicidal glimmer in my eyes, Méliès realizes there's no point in arguing. He lays me out on the workbench, the way Madeleine used to in the old days, and gets me to wait.

"Hold on, I'm going to find something for you."

I can't relax. My gears are making atrocious grating noises.

"I must have a few spare parts somewhere . . ." he adds.

"I'm fed up with being mended. I want something strong enough to withstand powerful emotions, like everybody else. Haven't you got a spare clock?"

"That won't solve anything. We need to mend your

flesh-and-blood heart. And you don't need a doctor or a clockmaker for that. You just need love, or time—but lots of time."

"I don't want to wait! I don't have any love left, so please, just change this clock for me."

Méliès heads into town to find me a new heart.

"Try to rest up until I'm back. And no silly business."

I decide to wind up my old heart one last time. My head is spinning. A guilty thought flies away to Madeleine, who made so many sacrifices for me to be able to stand on my own two feet and keep going forward without snapping. I feel thoroughly ashamed.

I thrust the key into my lock and a sharp pain rises up beneath my lungs. Drops of blood form at the intersection of my clock hands. I try to pull out the key, but it sticks in the lock. Then I try unjamming it with my broken clock hands. I force it, but my strength is fading fast. By the time I've finally succeeded, blood is pouring out of the lock. Curtain.

Méliès is back. I can only see a blurred mustache, you'd think my eyes had been replaced by Miss Acacia's.

"I found you a new heart—with no cuckoo and a much quieter tick-tock."

"Thank you . . ."

"Do you like it?"

"Yes, thank you . . ."

"You're quite sure you don't want the heart Madeleine saved your life with?"

"I'm sure."

"You'll never be the same again, you do understand?"

"That's exactly what I want."

I don't remember anything after that, except for a hazy dream, followed by a gigantic hangover.

chapter fourteen

In which much is revealed, but not necessarily resolved, concerning "The Man Who Was No Hoax"

When I finally open my eyes, I can see my old clock lying on the bedside table. It's odd being able to pick up your own heart. The cuckoo doesn't work anymore. And there's dust on it. I feel like a ghost leaning against a gravestone and calmly smoking a cigarette, except for the fact that I'm alive. I'm wearing a strange pair of pajamas and two tubes have been fitted into my veins—something else to drag around with me.

I inspect my new heart without clock hands. It doesn't make any noise. How long have I been asleep? Getting up is hard. My bones ache. Méliès is nowhere to be found. But there's a woman dressed in white sitting at his desk. His new *belle,* I guess. I wave at her. She looks startled, as if she's just seen an apparition. Her hands tremble. I think I might have frightened somebody at last.

"You've no idea how happy I am to see you back on your feet . . ."

"Me too. Where's Méliès?"

"Sit down, I need to explain a few things."

"I feel like I've been lying down for a hundred and fifty years, so standing up for five minutes isn't going to hurt me."

"Honestly, it's better if you sit down . . . I've got something important to tell you. Something nobody ever wanted to explain before."

"Where's Méliès?"

"He went back to Paris a few months ago. You've been asleep for a long time. He asked me to look after you. He loved you very much, you know. He was fascinated by the effect your clock had on your imagination. When you had your accident, he blamed himself terribly for not telling you about your true nature, even if he couldn't be certain whether doing so would have changed the course of events. But you need to know the truth, now."

"What accident?"

"Don't you remember?" she says sadly. "In Marbella, you tried to wrench out the clock that was stitched on to your heart."

"Oh yes . . ."

"Méliès tried to graft on a new heart, to cheer you up."

"Cheer me up? I was at death's door!"

"Yes, we all think we're going to die when we're separated from someone we love. But I'm talking about your heart in the mechanical sense of the word. Listen carefully, because I know you'll find what I'm about to say hard to believe . . ."

She sits down by my side and takes hold of my right hand. I can feel her trembling.

"You could have lived without either clock, old or new. They don't interact directly with your physical heart. They aren't real prosthetics, they're just placebos which, medically speaking, don't do anything."

"But that's impossible. Why would Madeleine have made all that up?"

"For psychological reasons, I expect. To protect you from her own demons, as many parents do, one way or another."

"Look, you don't understand this kind of medicine, it's as simple as that. At least now I realize why she always insisted I got my heart looked after by clockmakers and not doctors."

"I know it's a shock to wake up to this. But if you plan to live a real life at all, then you've got to stop getting wound up—if you'll forgive the pun—by all this nonsense."

"I don't believe you for a single second."

"And that's a perfectly normal reaction. You've believed in this cuckoo-clock heart story all your life."

"How do you know about my life?"

"I've read about it . . . Méliès wrote your story down in this book."

The Man Who Was No Hoax, it says on the cover. I leaf through it quickly: our epic journey across Europe; Granada; meeting up with Miss Acacia; Joe's comeback . . .

"Don't read the end right away," she admonishes me.

"Why not?"

"First, you need to get used to the idea that your life isn't linked to your clock. That's the only way for you to change the ending of this book."

"I could never believe that, let alone accept it."

"You lost Miss Acacia because of your iron belief in your wooden heart."

"I don't have to listen to this."

"You might have realized what was going on, if the story of your heart wasn't anchored so deeply inside you . . . But you must believe me now. Right, now you can go ahead and read the third section of the book, if you like, even though it'll be painful for you. One day, you'll be able to put all this behind you."

"Why did Méliès never tell me?"

"Méliès said you weren't ready to hear it yet, psychologically speaking. He deemed it too dangerous to reveal the truth to you on the evening of the 'accident,' given your state of shock by the time you'd made it back to the workshop. He blamed himself dreadfully for not having told you before . . . I think he got seduced by the idea of your cuckoo-clock heart. It doesn't take much for him to believe in the impossible. It cheered him up to watch you becoming a grown man with such complete belief . . . until that tragic night."

"I don't want those memories dredged up for the time being."

"I understand, but I do need to talk to you about what happened immediately afterward . . . Would you like something to drink?"

"Yes, please; but not alcohol, my head still hurts."

While the nurse goes in search of something to help me recover from my emotional overload, I look at my battered old heart on the bedside table, then the new clock under my crumpled pajamas. A metal dial, with clock hands protected by a pane of glass. A sort of bicycle bell sits on top of the number twelve. The clock feels scratchy, as if somebody else's heart has been grafted on to me. I wonder what that strange woman in white is going to try and make me believe next.

"While Méliès headed off into town that day, to find a clock that would temporarily calm you," she says, "you tried to wind up your broken clock. Do you remember that?"

"Yes, vaguely."

"From what Méliès described to me, you were virtually unconscious and bleeding heavily."

"Yes, my head was spinning, I could feel myself being dragged down . . ."

"You suffered internal bleeding. When Méliès realized this, he suddenly thought of his old friend, Jehanne d'Ancy, and came in great haste to find me. He might have forgotten my kisses all too quickly, but he always remembered my nursing talents. I was able to stem your hemorrhaging just in time, but you didn't regain consciousness. He still wanted to carry out the operation he'd promised you. He said you'd wake up in a better psychological state if you had a new clock. Call it an act of superstition on his part. He was terrified of you dying."

I listen to her tell my story; she could be giving me news about somebody I once dimly knew. It's difficult to connect these wild imaginings with my own reality.

"I was terribly in love with Méliès, even if it was unrequited. That was why I chose to take care of you at first, to stay in touch with him. Then I grew attached to your character as I read *The Man Who Was No Hoax*. I've been immersed in your story ever since, in every sense. I've watched over you from the day of your accident."

I'm completely taken aback. My blood is pumping strange lighthouse signals into the right side of my brain. *It could be true. It could be true.*

"According to Méliès, you destroyed your heart in front of Miss Acacia. You wanted to show her how much you were suffering, and at the same time how much you loved her. It was a rash and desperate act. But you were just a boy then—worse, a young man with childish dreams, who survived by muddling dreams and reality."

"I still was that childish teenager, until a few minutes ago . . ."

"No, that stopped when you decided to let go of your old heart. And that's precisely what Madeleine was frightened of: you growing up."

The more I repeat the word "impossible," the more "possible" it sounds inside my head.

"I'm only telling you what I've read about you in the book Méliès wrote. He gave it to me just before setting off for Paris."

I open the book again. I read how, while I was sleeping, letters arrived for me from Edinburgh. That Méliès wrote to Dr. Madeleine to explain everything that had happened. But the letter that came back was penned by Arthur. Then I read the news that, secretly, I had always been half dreading:

The morning that Little Jack left us, Luna, Anna and I returned to the top of the mountain to find the door to the house half-open and no one in sight. Madeleine's workshop was destroyed. You'd think a storm had just swept through it. All of her boxes had been opened and even the cat had gone.

We set off in search of Madeleine, finally tracking her down to St. Calford's prison. During the few minutes we had with her, she explained that the police had arrested her just after our departure, but that we shouldn't worry, it wasn't the first time she'd been locked up, and everything would sort itself out in the end.

I'd like to be able to write that she was released, I'd

like to be able to tell you that she cooks with one hand while mending somebody with the other, and that, even though she misses Little Jack, she's bearing up. But later that same day Madeleine left us. She set out on a journey from which she'll never return. She left her body behind in prison and set her heart free.

I know this news will hit Little Jack hard. But, dear Méliès, I must ask you to let him know that even in the depths of sadness, he must never forget that he gave Madeleine the joy of being a real mother. That was her life's dream. You know what I mean?

We sent the news by Luna's pigeon, but when the letter got lost our nerve failed us. Bloody bird! That Jack still believed Madeleine to be alive was too much for us to bear, but we weren't yet strong enough to tell him the truth. And now Jack is also sleeping . . . Oh, Méliès, I'll try not to reread this letter, otherwise I might never have the courage to send it to you.

Anna, Luna and I wish Little Jack all the strength he needs to recover from his ordeals, and hope that he will one day understand Madeleine's—and our—need to shield him from the wicked world.

Arthur

PS—Don't forget to sing "When the Saints Go Marching In!" to Little Jack.

Silence.

"When is Méliès coming back?"

"I don't think he'll ever come back. He's the father of two children now, and he's working hard on his idea of photography in motion."

"A father? How much time has passed to make Méliès a father? And for me to have lost my Madeleine-mother?"

"To start with, he used to write to the two of us every week. Now, whole months can go by without me hearing any news; I think he fears I'll have to announce . . . your death."

"What do you mean, whole months?"

"It's the fourth of August, 1892. You've been asleep for nearly three years. I know you won't want to believe that. But just look at yourself in the mirror. Your long hair is a measure of how much time has gone by."

"I don't want to look at anything just now. There's too much to take in as it is."

"During the first three months, you used to open your eyes for a few seconds a day at most. Then one day you woke up and uttered the odd word about Dr. Madeleine or Miss Acacia, before returning to your state."

The mere mention of their names stirs up feelings that are contradictory, but stronger than ever.

"Since the beginning of the year, your periods of wakefulness have become longer and more regular. Right up until today. People do wake up from long comas like yours. After all, it's just a very long night of sleep. What an unexpected joy to see you standing on your feet at last. Méliès will be beside himself . . . But be warned, you might experience a few aftereffects."

"Meaning?"

"No one comes back from such a long journey unscathed; as it is, it's remarkable you can remember who you are."

I catch my reflection in the glazed workshop door. Three years. And Dr. Madeleine no longer of this world. Three years. I'm one of the living dead. What have you done with these three years, Miss Acacia?

"Am I really alive, is this a dream, a nightmare, or am I dead?"

"You're very much alive; different, but alive."

Once I've got rid of those horrible tubes pinching the hairs on my arms, I try to gather my wits and emotions as I eat my first proper meal.

Miss Acacia has taken over my thoughts. So I can't be doing too badly. I'm as obsessed by her as I was on my tenth birthday. I've got to find her. I can't be sure about anything anymore, except the one thing that matters: I still love her. Just thinking about her being apart from me stokes my fiery nausea. Nothing makes any sense if I don't try to find her.

It's not even a choice. I have to go back to the Extraordinarium.

"You can't go there like that!"

But I set off in the direction of town without finishing my meal. I've never run so slowly. The fresh air in my lungs feels like gusts of steel. I could be a hundred years old.

On the outskirts of Granada, great cauldrons of ochre dust are whipped up so that the whitewashed houses seem to blur into the sky. I see my own shadow in a small street but I don't recognize it; nor do I recognize the new reflection that bounces off a window pane. With my shaggy locks and beard, I look like Father Christmas before he got a big belly and white hair. But that's not all. My aching bones have changed the way I walk. My shoulders seem to have expanded, and these shoes hurt my feet, as if they're too small for me now. Children hide under their mothers' skirts when they see me.

At a bend in the street, I happen upon a poster starring Miss Acacia. I stare at it for a long time, trembling with melancholic desire. Her gaze has grown more self-assured, although she still doesn't wear glasses. Her nails are longer, and she paints them now. Miss Acacia is more ravishing than ever, while I've turned into a caveman in pajamas.

When I get to the Extraordinarium I head straight for the Ghost Train. My favorite memories rush up at me, finding their place again inside my head. Unhappy memories don't waste any time in joining them.

I'm taking a seat in one of the carriages when, all of a sudden, I notice Joe. He's sitting on the landing, smoking a cigarette. The ride appears to have been extended. Suddenly . . . I can see Miss Acacia, sitting a few rows behind me. Be quiet, my heart. She doesn't recognize me. Be quiet, my heart. Nobody recognizes me. Quite frankly, I'm having a hard time recognizing myself. Joe tries to frighten me the way he does the other passengers. He won't succeed. That said, when I see him kiss Miss Acacia at the exit to the Ghost Train, I know his talents for trampling on other people's dreams are alive and kicking. But I won't be discouraged, not this time. Because now I'm the one who's the Outsider.

Miss Acacia takes a puff of Joe's cigarette. The intimacy this implies makes me feel as sick as seeing them kiss. They're only a few meters away. I hold my breath.

He kisses her again; the way you might roll up your sleeves and do the washing up. How can you kiss a girl like that without thinking about it? I don't say anything. Give her back to me! You'll see how much heart I'll put into it, whatever that heart might be made of. I'm all shaken up, and it takes every bit of strength I've got to hold my emotions in check.

Her sparkling voice, like strawberry-flavored tear gas, stings my eyes. Will she ever recognize me?

Am I strong enough to tell her the truth this time, and if it goes wrong, am I strong enough to hide it from her?

Joe goes back inside the Ghost Train. Miss Acacia walks past me. The wreaths of her perfume are as familiar as an old bedcover full of dreams. I could almost forget she's the lover of my bitter enemy.

"Hello," she says, noticing me. My shoulders sink under the dead weight of her nonrecognition. I notice a bruise on her left knee.

I dive straight in, without really knowing what I'm doing.

"Still not wearing your glasses, then?"

"No, but I don't like people teasing me about it," she says with a relieved smile.

"I know . . ."

"What do you mean, you know?"

I know we fought because of Joe and jealousy, I know I threw my heart away because I loved you crookedly, but I want to learn everything afresh because I love you more than all the world. There you go, that's what I should have said. The words flit across my mind and head for my mouth, but they don't come out. I just cough instead.

"Why are you wearing your pajamas outside? You haven't run away from hospital, have you?"

She talks to me gently, as if I were an old man.

"I didn't run away . . . I've come back from a very serious illness . . ."

"Well, Señor, you're going to need some clothes now!"

We smile at each other, the way we used to. For a moment, I think she's worked out who I am, or at least that's what I secretly wish for. "See you soon," we say, and I head back to Méliès's workshop with a sort of twisted hope.

"Don't put off revealing your true identity," the nurse insists.

"I need a bit longer, the time to get used to her again."

"Well, don't take too long about it . . . You've already lost her once by hiding your past. Otherwise she'll bury her head in your chest, only to discover there's another clock in place of the old one. Speaking of which, why don't I get rid of it once and for all?"

"Look, we will get rid of it, but I need more time. It was Dr. Madeleine's masterpiece, after all. Let's just wait until I'm feeling a bit better, all right?"

"You're feeling better already . . . How about I cut your hair and shave off that prehistoric beard of yours?"

"No, not yet. By the way, you don't happen to have one of Méliès's old suits still hanging around?"

Every now and then, I position myself in a key spot, not far from the Ghost Train. That way, we can run into each other, as if by chance. The rapport we strike up resembles what we used to have so closely that I don't know if I'm laughing or crying. Sometimes, during our silences, I tell myself that she knows but isn't saying anything. Except that's not her style.

I'm careful not to harass Miss Acacia. I've learned my lesson from my first accident in love. Instinctively, I still want to push things, but the pain slows me down; or at any rate stops me being in such a rush.

I'm starting to manipulate the truth again. But I'm enjoying nibbling the crumbs of her presence from the safety of my new identity, and the thought of ending all this makes my stomach lurch.

This game has been going on for more than two months and Joe doesn't seem to have noticed anything. Méliès's shoes are starting to hurt my feet now. As for his suit, I look like I'm going fishing disguised as a magician. Jehanne, my nurse, thinks this metamorphosis is a result of my long coma. My bones are trying to make up for lost time after being compacted like springs for three years. As a result, I've got curvature of the spine, which affects my whole body. Even my face is changing. My jaw is more thickset, and my cheekbones more prominent.

"Here comes Mr. Neander-Cute dressed up in his brand-new suit," Miss Acacia calls out when she sees me coming. "All you need is a trip to the hairdresser's and we'll have you back to being a fully civilized man," she tells me today.

"If you call me Mr. Neander-Cute, I'll never shave my beard off again."

It came out just like that, *dragando piano,* as Méliès might whisper.

"You could shave it off, and I'd still call you Mr. Neander-Cute, if you'd like . . ."

So we're back to these deliciously confused emotions. I can't savor them fully but it's already a lot better than being apart from her.

"You remind me of an old lover I once had."

"More of the 'old' or the 'lover'?"

"Both."

"Did he have a beard?"

"No, but he was a mysterious figure like you. He

believed in his lies, or rather his dreams. I thought it was just to impress me, but he really did believe in them."

"Perhaps he believed in them and wanted to impress you at the same time."

"Perhaps . . . I don't know. He died a few years back."

"Died?"

"Yes, I laid flowers on his grave again this morning."

"And what if he only died to impress you, to get you to believe in him?"

"Oh, he'd have been perfectly capable of something like that, but he wouldn't have waited three years to come back."

"What did he die of?"

"That's a mystery. Some people saw him struggling with a horse, others say that he died in a fire which he accidentally started. As for me, I'm afraid he died in a fit of anger after our final argument. It was a terrible row. All I know for sure is that he's dead, because they buried him. And anyway if he was alive, he'd be *here*. With me."

A ghost hiding behind his beard, that's what I've become.

"Did he love you too much?"

"You can never love someone too much."

"Did he love you badly?"

"I don't know . . . But let me tell you this: encouraging me to talk about my first love, who died three years ago, isn't the best way of flirting with me."

"What is the best way of flirting with you, then?"

"Not to flirt with me."

"I knew it. That's exactly why I haven't been flirting with you!"

She smiled.

I nearly, so nearly, told her everything. With my old heart, it would have popped out all by itself . . . but now, everything's different.

I went back to the workshop just as a vampire reclaims his coffin—ashamed of having bitten a magnificent neck.

You'll never be the same again, Méliès told me before the operation. Regrets and remorse press against a stormy gulf. Only a few months have gone by and I'm already fed up with my life in its muted version. I've finished convalescing now, and want to return to the heat of the fire without this mask of a beard and bushy hair. I don't mind growing up a bit, and I've got to turn this false reunion around.

Tonight, when I go to bed, I'm eager to rummage among the memories and dreams that lie in passion's dustbin. I want to see what's left of my old heart, the one that let me fall in love last time.

My new clock hardly makes any noise, but I'm no less of an insomniac. The old one is tidied away on a shelf, in a cardboard box. Perhaps if I repaired it, everything would be just as it was before. No Joe, no knife between the clock hands. To travel back in time to that period when I loved guilelessly, when I forged my way, head down, without worrying about bumping into my dreams. Bring back those days when I wasn't afraid of anything; when I could climb on board love's rose-tinted rocket without fastening my safety belt. I'm older, today, and more sensible too; but as a result, I no longer dare leap toward the woman who'll always make me feel like I'm ten years old. My old heart will continue to make me dream more than the new one, even though it's battered and outside my body now. It's the "real thing"; it's mine. And like a fool, I went and smashed it. What have I become? My own impostor? A see-through shadow?

I grab the cardboard box and carefully take out the clock, putting it down on my bed. Curls of dust rise up. I slide my fingers inside my former gears. Pain, or the memory of that pain, is instantly revived; followed by a surprisingly comforting feeling.

After a few seconds, the clock goes clickety-clack, like a skeleton learning to walk again, then it stops. My rapture transports me from the top of Arthur's Seat into the tender arms of Miss Acacia. I tie the clock hands back in position with two pieces of string; it's not a very sturdy arrangement.

I spend the night trying to repair my old wooden heart; but being the pathetic tinkerer I am, I don't have any luck. If only Madeleine were here, to flash that twitch of a smile before expertly manipulating my clock gears. Or Méliès, with all his sound advice. But by dawn, I've made up my own mind. I'm going to find Miss Acacia to tell her the whole truth. I've put my old clock back in the box. It's a present for someone who has become a great singer. I won't just give her the key this time, I'll give her the whole heart too, in the hope that she might once again decide to tinker at love with me.

I walk down the main avenue in the Extraordinarium, like someone condemned to die. I cross paths with Joe, and our eyes meet as if we're fighting a duel in a western, in slow motion.

But I'm not afraid anymore. For the first time in my life, I imagine what it must be like to be in his shoes. Today I'm in a position to win back Miss Acacia, just as he was when he took on the job at the Ghost Train. I think about how much he must have hated me at school when I couldn't stop talking about her, not realizing that he was in agony because she'd gone away and never come back. This great tall fellow and I almost have something in common. I watch him stride off until he disappears out of sight.

Up on the Ghost Train walkway, Brigitte Heim appears. When I catch sight of her hairstyle, identical to the bristles on a broom, I turn back. She's like a sallow witch who reeks of loneliness; and as unhappy as those piles of old stones she collects. I could have tried talking calmly to her, now that she no longer recognizes me. But just the idea of her spitting spiteful remarks makes me feel tired.

Miss Acacia, or the gift of ensuring things never work out quite as they were planned . . .

"I've got something to tell you."

"Me too."

"I don't think it's a good idea for us to carry on . . . Oh, you've got a present for me? What's inside the box?"

"A heart in a thousand pieces. Mine . . ."

"You're pretty single-minded, for somebody who's not meant to be flirting with me."

"Forget about the impostor you saw yesterday. I want to tell you the whole truth now."

"The truth is you never stop trying to flirt, with your unkempt appearance and that suit you wear. And I'll admit it works for me . . . a tiny bit."

I grab her cheeks between my fingers. They've lost none of their glow. I place my lips on hers without saying a word. The softness of her lips makes me momentarily forget my best intentions. I wonder if I didn't just hear a clickety-clack from inside the box. The kiss leaves me with an aftertaste of red peppers. A second kiss takes over from the first. We press harder this time, plugging back into electric memories, reconnecting with treasures buried deep beneath the skin. *Robber! Impostor!* hisses the right side of my brain. *Wait! Let's talk about it later,* my body answers. My heart is being tugged in opposite directions; it beats wildly with all its might. I'm intoxicated by the pure and simple joy of rediscovering her, despite the nasty feeling that I'm also cuckolding myself. This kind of simultaneous happiness and suffering is too much. I'm used to rain after fine weather. But right now, flashes of lightning are streaking across the bluest sky in the world.

"I asked to speak first . . ." she tells me sadly, extricating herself from my embrace. "I don't want to carry on seeing you. I know we've been circling around each other for months now, but I'm in love with someone else, and have been for a long time. It would be crazy to start a new relationship, I'm really sorry. But I'm still in love . . ."

"With Joe, I know."

"No, with Jack, the old lover I told you about, the one you remind me of sometimes."

A big bang of sensations wreaks havoc with my emotional connections. Tears come without warning, hot and long, impossible to hold back.

"I'm sorry, I didn't want to hurt you, but I've already married someone I'm not in love with. I can't start all over again," she says, putting her slim arms around me.

My eyelashes must be spitting rainbows.

"I can't accept a present from you. I'm really sorry. Don't make things any more complicated than they already are."

I take my courage in both hands as I grab hold of the parcel containing my clockwork heart. "Open it anyway, it's a present intended for you alone. If you don't take it, nobody else can use it."

She accepts, visibly embarrassed. Her carefully painted pretty little fingers tear off the paper. She feigns a smile. It's a precious moment. Giving your heart wrapped up in a box to the woman of your life is no small undertaking.

She shakes the box, going through the motions of guessing its contents.

"Is it fragile?"

"Yes, it's fragile."

Her discomfort is palpable. Gently, she lifts the lid. Her hands dive to the bottom of the box and grab hold of my old clockwork heart. The top of the dial appears in the daylight, then the center of the clock and its clock hands that have been stuck together again.

She looks at it. Not a word. She rummages nervously in her handbag, gets out a pair of glasses, which she clumsily perches on her tiny nose. Her eyes scrutinize every detail. She makes the clock hands turn clockwise and then anticlockwise. Her spectacles mist up on the outside. She shakes her head slowly. Her lenses mist up on the inside too. Her hands are trembling; they're attached to the inside of my chest. My body registers their seismic movements and reproduces them even though, technically speaking, she's not touching me. My clocks ring out inside me, shaken by the trembling that grows stronger all the time.

Miss Acacia gently puts my heart down on the low wall that we snuggled up against so many times. Finally, she raises her head in my direction.

Her lips part and whisper:

"Every day, I went there every single day. I've been laying flowers on your bloody grave for three years. From the day you were buried until this morning. I was there again only just now. But that was the last time . . . Because from now on, as far as I'm concerned, you no longer exist . . ."

∙   ∙   ∙

She turns on her heel for good and steps slowly over the wall. My clockwork heart is still lying on top of it, clock hands pointing to the ground. Miss Acacia's gaze passes right through me. She doesn't even look angry; it really is as if I don't exist anymore. Her gaze is like a sad bird, hovering for a moment over the cardboard box, then flying off toward skies I'll never know. The pitter-patter of her footsteps fades. Soon, I'll no longer be able to see her voluptuous derrière rolling in a velvet backwash. The swish of her skirt will have vanished; and only a hint of her soft tread will linger on. She'll be just ten centimeters tall. Nine centimeters, six, scarcely the size of an empty matchbox. Five, four, three, two . . .

This time, I'll never, ever see her again.

Epilogue

Dr. Madeleine's clockwork heart continued its journey outside our hero's body, if we can call him a hero.

Brigitte Heim was the first to notice it. On a low wall, the cuckoo-clock heart looked like a toy offered to the dead. She picked it up, to add to her collection of unusual objects. And so the clock lay for a while between two ancient skulls, on the floor of the Ghost Train.

On the day that Joe recognized it, he lost his powers as a Scareperson. One night, after his performance, he decided to get rid of it. He took the road toward the cemetery of San Felipe, with the clock under his arm. Whether as a mark of respect or whether out of pure superstition we'll never know, but he laid the clock down on Little Jack's untended grave.

Miss Acacia left the Extraordinarium during the month of October 1892. On that same day in October, the clock disappeared from the cemetery of San Felipe. Joe continued with his Ghost Train career, haunted to the end of his days by the loss of Miss Acacia.

Performing under her grandmother's name, Miss Acacia went on to set hearts alight in cabarets across Europe. Ten years later, when she came to Paris, she could have been spotted in a cinema that was screening *Voyage to the Moon* by one Georges Méliès, who had become cinema's greatest precursor, its inventor par excellence. Had they met, they would have conversed in hushed tones for a few minutes after the screening. He would have given her a copy of *The Man Who Was No Hoax*.

A week later, the clock resurfaced on the doormat of an old Edinburgh house. It was wrapped in a shroud, as if a stork (or a pigeon) had just dropped it off.

The heart remained on the doormat for several hours before being picked up by Anna and Luna—who had reoccupied the deserted house, founding a different sort of orphanage that looked after older children too, such as Arthur. After Madeleine's death, rust had invaded Arthur's spine. The slightest movement made him creak. He grew afraid of the cold and the rain. The clock came to the end of its journey on his bedside table, together with the book that was tucked inside the parcel.

Jehanne d'Ancy, Little Jack's nurse in Granada, never

saw that clock again, but eventually found the way to Méliès's heart. They spent the rest of their days together, running a shop specializing in pranks and hoaxes close to Montparnasse station. The world had forgotten about Méliès by then, but Jehanne continued to listen passionately to his stories about the man with the cuckoo-clock heart and other shadowy monsters.

As for our "hero," he grew taller and taller. But he never got over the loss of Miss Acacia. He went out every night, only at night, to roam the outskirts of the Extraordinarium, in the shadow of its fairground attractions. But the half-ghost that he had become never crossed its threshold.

Then he retraced his own boyish footsteps all the way back to Edinburgh. The city was exactly as he remembered it; time seemed to have stood still there. He climbed Arthur's Seat, just as he had as a child. Great big snowflakes landed on his shoulders, heavy as corpses. The wind licked the old volcano from head to toe, its frozen tongue goring the mist. It wasn't the coldest day on earth, but it wasn't far off either. Deep inside the blizzard, the pitter-patter of footsteps rang out. On the right-hand side of the volcano, he thought he recognized a familiar figure. He saw wind-tousled hair, and that distinctive strut of a proud doll prone to bumping into things. Just another dream I've got muddled with reality, he said to himself.

When he pushed open the door of his childhood home, all of Madeleine's clocks were silent. Anna and Luna, his two garishly dressed aunts, had great difficulty in recognizing this person who could no longer properly be called "Little Jack." He had to sing a few notes of "Oh When the Saints" before they opened their skinny arms. Although he already knew the story, Luna gently explained to him how Méliès had written to "Dr. Madeleine," informing her of Little Jack's coma, only to receive a reply from Arthur instead. In it, the bed-bound former tramp laid out the details of his original letter, the one that had never reached Jack, but which Méliès would include in *The Man Who Was No Hoax*. And Luna also owned up to the fact that the other letters sent by bird had been written by her and Anna. Before the silence could make the walls explode, Anna took Jack's hand very firmly in hers and led him to Arthur's bedside.

The old man revealed the secret of Little Jack's life to him:

"Without Madeleine's clock, you would never have survived the coldest day on earth. But after a few months, your flesh and blood heart was strong enough. She could have removed the clock, as expertly as she removed stitches. That's what she should have done. You know what I mean?

"No family dared adopt you because of that tick-tock contraption sticking out of your left rib. But over time, she grew attached. Madeleine saw you as a tiny fragile thing to be protected at all costs, linked to her by an umbilical cord in the form of a cuckoo clock.

"She was terribly afraid of the day when you'd become

an adult. She tried to adjust your heart so that she could always keep you close to her. She promised us she'd try and get used to the idea you might also suffer in love one day, because that's how life is. You know what I mean?

"But she never did."

AUTHOR'S NOTE

MY CHARACTER GEORGES MÉLIÈS is inspired by the original Méliès (1861–1938, the first cinematographic director, father of special effects), who himself was heavily influenced by Jean-Eugène Robert-Houdin (1805–1871)—a remarkable man with an extraordinary gift for invention. He was a clockmaker and illusionist, and inventor of, among other things, the kilometric counter and ophthalmological equipment. He established a theater where he made clocks embellished with singing birds and other examples of mechanical prowess. The infamous magician "Houdini" chose his patronymic in honor of his forerunner.

ACKNOWLEDGMENTS

FOR THE UPKEEP, fine-tuning and wonderful turns of the key given to the clockwork heart of this book, thanks to Olivia de Dieuleveult and Olivia Ruiz.

A Note About the Author

Mathias Malzieu is the lead singer of the French rock band
Dionysos. *The Boy with the Cuckoo-Clock Heart* is the basis for
an album that Malzieu wrote; and he will codirect an ani-
mated feature film adaptation, which has been optioned by
Luc Besson. This is his third novel and the first to be translated into English. Born in 1974 in Montpellier, Malzieu now
lives in Paris.

A NOTE ON THE TYPE

This book was set in Celeste, a typeface created in 1994 by the designer Chris Burke. He describes it as a modern, humanistic face having less contrast between thick and thin strokes than other modern types such as Bodoni, Didot, and Walbaum. Tempered by some old-style traits and with a contemporary, slightly modular letterspacing, Celeste is highly readable and especially adapted for current digital printing processes that render an increasingly exacting letterform.

Composed by Creative Graphics, Allentown, Pennsylvania

Printed and bound by RR Donnelley, Harrisonburg, Virginia

Designed by Maggie Hinders